SOPHIE HARTLEY, ON STRIKE

Stephanie Greene

sandpiper

Houghton Mifflin Harcourt
Boston New York

www.hmhbooks.com

The text of this book is set in 13-point Giovanni Book.

Cover photographs: (soccer ball) © Le Do/Shutterstock, (blocks) © Johann Helgason/Shutterstock,
(sunglasses) © Maria Dryfhout/Shutterstock, (army men) © JF Trice/Shutterstock, (ballet slippers)
© CLM/Shutterstock, (lamb) © Dorling Kindersley/Getty Images, (basket) © Blend Images/Veer.

Cover design by Sharismar Rodriguez

The Library of Congress has cataloged the hardcover edition as follows:
Greene, Stephanie.
Sophie Hartley, on strike / by Stephanie Greene.
p. cm.
Summary: After their mother sets up a new list of household chores for them,
Sophie and her siblings argue about housekeeping and finally go on strike.
[1. Family life—Fiction. 2. Housekeeping—Fiction.] I. Title.
PZ7.G8434Sop 2006
[Fic]—dc22   2006008375

ISBN: 978-0-618-71960-0 hardcover
ISBN: 978-0-547-55018-3 paperback

Manufactured in the United States of America
DOM 10 9 8 7 6 5 4 3 2 1

4500297039

To my mother

CHAPTER ONE

If Sophie hadn't stopped to watch television with John on Saturday morning but had gone straight to the kitchen and written a note saying she was going to Alice's house, she might have been able to slip out the back door before her mother came down. The Hartley family wouldn't have gotten into such a mess later on, either.

But it was one of Sophie's favorite TV programs. Even though she'd seen it a million times, she couldn't resist. It put her totally off schedule.

"Oh, no, you don't," said Mrs. Hartley, coming into the kitchen as Sophie was opening the back door. She had Maura on one hip and the bucket of household cleaning supplies resting on the other. "Where do you think *you're* going?" She plopped Maura in her high chair and put the bucket on the floor next to the sink. "Have you cleaned your room yet?" she said, turning to Sophie with a knowing look.

Sophie vowed never to watch TV again. There was a small window of opportunity in which a person could escape from the Hartley house on a Saturday morning before Mrs. Hartley appeared and started assigning chores, and Sophie had missed it. Horrible chores that wasted the entire morning, like dusting tables and sweeping the mudroom floor and other totally unnecessary tasks. What was the point of cleaning the house when it was only going to get dirty again?

Sophie eyed the distance from the back porch to the garage longingly. She could probably be on her bike and down the driveway before her mother made it to the door. But when she tried to imagine what it would be like when she came home, all she could see was black.

"Alice invited me over," she said, one hand on the doorknob and the other clutching the strap of her bicycle helmet.

"You can go to Alice's when your jobs are done." Her mother poured some dry cereal on the tray of the highchair and handed Maura a cup with a lid. "First, you need to strip your bed, put on clean sheets, and vacuum your room."

"Thad went out without doing *his* room," said Sophie.

"Thad has soccer practice."

"What about Nora?"

"Nora's asleep." Her mother put her mug of coffee on the table and sat down. "All you have to worry about is yourself."

"I don't see why I have to work when no one else is," Sophie insisted stubbornly. "John is watching TV, and look at Maura. She's making a mess and she doesn't even have to clean it up."

It was true. There was more dry cereal on the floor around Maura's highchair than on her tray, and the pieces there were floating in a pool of juice like miniature life preservers. Maura slapped the pool with her hand and laughed.

Mrs. Hartley expertly grabbed her hand while sopping up the juice with the towel she kept over her shoulder for such emergencies. Then she took away Maura's cup and handed her a piece of banana. Maura immediately crammed it into her mouth.

"I'll make Maura mop the floor the minute she learns how to walk," Mrs. Hartley said. "I promise."

"It's not funny." Sophie reluctantly hung her helmet back on its hook next to the door. She was sick of the way Maura got out of doing everything just because she was a baby. And Thad because he played sports. And Nora because she needed her "beauty sleep," as she called it. It wasn't fair.

"Why doesn't John have to strip his bed?" she asked.

"John is six," said her mother. "When you were six, you didn't change your bed, either. For heaven's sake, Sophie! You could've finished your chores and been at Alice's house by now if you stopped worrying about what everybody else is doing."

It was impossible for Sophie not to worry. She felt as if she was always the one who ended up doing chores on Saturday morning. All by herself, too. It wouldn't be so bad if they were all moaning and groaning and vacuuming together. At least they'd be doing something as a family. They could turn it into a fun family time, and have pillow fights and tie their dirty sheets together to practice fire drills from their bedroom windows.

Sometimes it felt as if they hardly ever did things as a family anymore. Sophie missed it. Now that Thad was in high school, he always seemed to be at some sort of practice, and Nora skinned out of everything by sleeping late on the weekends. Sophie had tried sleeping late, too. But even after she made herself lie in bed with her eyes shut for what felt like a million hours, it was never later than seven thirty when she finally looked at the clock.

"I can't strip my bed now," she said with a

half-hearted display of sisterly love. "I don't want to wake up Nora."

"You can start in the living room, then," her mother said, "and dust the tables and straighten the magazines and basically make the room more livable. I shouldn't have to tell you what to do all the time. You know what needs to be done. Unless, of course," she added sweetly, looking at Sophie's stormy brow, "you'd rather do the bathrooms."

It really wasn't that hard a job, once she got started. Sophie slid the magazines under the couch and gave the coffee table a cursory wipe with the hem of her T-shirt. She picked up an armful of the assorted shoes people had left lying around and, after carefully placing hers, and a pair of her father's, side by side in the front hall closet, put one of each of the other pairs in with them. The rest she dumped in a pile in the mudroom.

Thinking about how Thad and Nora and John were going to have to look all over the house to make a matching pair cheered

Sophie up so much, she decided to plump up the pillows on the couch as a bonus. A dense fog of dust rose out of them as soon as she started, so she stopped. Really! she thought fussily as she put them back. You'd think someone would take them outside and beat them once in a while.

"I'm done!" she shouted, and headed for the stairs. All she had to do now was strip her bed. Too bad for Nora if it woke her up. Maybe she'd get a pimple because her beauty sleep was cut short.

Nora hated pimples. She had an absolute fit whenever she got one, and spent hours trying to erase it with sticks and cover it with makeup. Sometimes, she wore little round patches on her face all night to make them disappear.

Once, she woke up with one on the tip of her nose and refused to go to school. Sophie hadn't blamed her. It had been impossible to look at anything else on Nora's face. Everyone at school would have gone cross-eyed talking to her.

Sophie didn't understand why Nora even got pimples if she hated them so much. Sophie was never going to get them. She was going to have a clear, spotless face for her whole life and drive Nora crazy.

John was still lying on his stomach in front of the TV with his eyes glued to the program and his feet in his yellow rubber boots tapping in time to the music. Here she was, working her fingers to the bone, and John got to lie there like Little Lord Fauntleroy, doing nothing. Sophie loved the book about the little boy who was poor until he found out he was an earl and went to live in a mansion in England. Sophie planned on being a queen herself, some day. But there wasn't room for royalty in the Hartley family now. Especially not on Saturday morning.

"Mom said you have to strip your bed," she told him.

"Did not," said John.

"Did, too."

John didn't bother turning around.

"Only *babies* don't have to strip their beds,"

Sophie said, and continued up the stairs. She stomped down the hall to her room as loudly as she could and threw open her bedroom door, letting it bang against the wall, but it was all wasted. The room was empty. Nora's bed had been neatly made. The dirty sheets were already in a pile on the rug along with Nora's dirty clothes.

No fair! thought Sophie grumpily as she plunked down on the edge of her bed. First, Nora got to sleep late. Then, when she woke up and realized it was Saturday, she got to be happy.

Nora loved cleaning their room. Or, at least, her side of their room. Every week, she used her mother's feather duster on her lamp shade, lemon oil on her dresser, and ammonia and water on the full-length mirror on the back of the closet door. By the time she was finished, their room smelled like the inside of the cabinet under the kitchen sink where Mrs. Hartley kept the cleaning products.

Nora had read somewhere that if you put perfume on a light bulb it made the whole room smell when you turned on the light, so now their room stunk whenever Nora was doing her homework, too. Sophie had complained that the fumes were giving her a headache, but all her mother did was tell her to open her window.

Sophie plucked at one of the many loose threads on her old bedspread until it snapped.

That was another thing.

For a long time, she and Nora had had matching bedspreads. Then Nora bought herself a colorful paisley spread with beads and sequins all over it—and pillows to match—with the money she made baby-sitting. Now Nora's bed looked like the "after" picture in a magazine, and Sophie's looked like the "before."

Nora was a fanatic about the dumb spread. She folded it back carefully every night before she got into bed, and had an absolute fit if anyone even sat on it.

A few weeks before, when Mrs. Hartley had been trying again to discourage John from his idea of joining the army, she had told him that if he became a soldier he was going to have to make his bed so that the inspecting officer could bounce a coin off his blanket. All John said was, "I'll take Nora with me. That's how she makes her bed."

Sophie was thinking about bouncing something heavier off Nora's bed—like a book, maybe, or the lamp—when Nora came sailing back into the room with her hair wet from the shower.

"Don't even think about it," she said with a quick flick of her hair. "That spread needs to be dry-cleaned. If I see one fingerprint, you're going to pay for it."

Sophie stood up and tugged listlessly at her sheets. "What?" she protested. "I'm making my bed."

"You are so *transparent*," Nora said in a superior voice as she bent to pick up her dirty laundry. "I'm going down to get the vacuum cleaner. You can use it when I'm through and take it back."

"Transparent" is what Nora called everyone these days. The French teacher who gave Nora a C because he was jealous of her superior French accent was transparent; the boy who sat behind her in English class and threw things at her because he was trying to flirt with her was transparent. She had even called Mr. Hartley transparent one night at dinner during their weekly argument, and had been sent away from the table.

Sophie could tell it was an insult by Nora's voice. She had her mother write the word down so she could look it up in the dictionary and learned it meant "easy to see through" or "obvious." That's exactly what Sophie had thought it meant.

"You're not the boss of me," she said to Nora's back.

"Like a shallow pool . . ." Nora said airily as she drifted from the room.

"You be quiet," Sophie said crossly.

That was one more thing Nora had started doing since she turned thirteen: uttering seemingly harmless phrases at Sophie over and over again—always when there was no grown-up around to hear them—until they became insults. Sophie didn't like it one bit. It didn't hurt as much as the kicking and hitting she and Nora used to do, but it was much more annoying. Not only was it hard to combat, it was almost impossible to get Nora in trouble.

". . . and then she called me a shallow pool," Sophie had told her parents indignantly the first time Nora said it. "You need to punish her."

"Those are harsh words," her father agreed solemnly. "What do you think?" he said to Mrs. Hartley, sitting across the room on the couch. "Is it the guillotine for old Nora?"

"That's far too good for her," said Mrs. Hartley.

The way they laughed together had made it even worse.

Sophie pulled her bedspread up over her week-old sheets and got a clean pillowcase out of the linen closet in the hall to substitute it for her old one. Her mother had taken to sniffing Sophie's pillow every week, even when Sophie swore she'd stripped her sheets.

Someone must have ratted and told Mrs. Hartley that Sophie only changed her sheets once a month. *Someone* being Nora.

Her bed finished, Sophie sat down on the edge and, balancing on her elbows, leaned back and stretched her legs across the space between the two beds to do a light tap dance on the edge of Nora's spread with her bare feet.

Nora had said no fingerprints. She didn't say anything about feet.

When Sophie arrived at Alice's house, she found out that Alice and her mother had gone shopping.

"You just missed them," Alice's dad told her cheerfully, as if knowing how close she had come was supposed to make Sophie feel better. Hearing that her other friend, Jenna, had gone with them made matters even worse.

Sophie pedaled furiously back home to complain. After she put her bike in the garage and started for the house, though, she heard the vacuum cleaner roaring. Knowing that her mother would only give her more jobs to do if she went inside, she spent the rest of the morning swinging on the rusty boring swing and looking for interesting junk in the garage. When she finally heard the vacuum cleaner stop, she knew it was safe to go in.

By then, unfortunately, Thad had made himself three sandwiches and eaten the last of the ham and cheese. All that was left for her lunch was one slice of white bread and the end piece of whole wheat.

"I thought you were having lunch at Alice's," her mother said in response to Sophie's loud objections.

"She was gone by the time I got there," said Sophie.

"Well?" said Mrs. Hartley. "And whose fault was that?"

Sophie was now eating a peanut butter and jelly sandwich on two-toned bread and watching her mother peer into the refrigerator to see what she needed to buy at the grocery store. Sophie didn't dare say out loud how bored she was; she knew she'd find herself pushing the grocery cart and being told over and over again to "put that back."

She wished her father was at home. Shopping with him was much more fun. He let them buy all kinds of things Mrs. Hartley wouldn't dream of buying, like sugar-coated cereal and chocolate milk in cartons.

Better yet, if he was home, he'd park his massive moving truck in the driveway and let her play in the van. Thad liked to skateboard down the ramp, and before Nora got too old, she and Sophie used to take the empty refrigerator and dishwasher boxes and the heavy quilted pads their father protected the furniture with and put on plays. If the truck had been out there now, Sophie could have made up a play for Alice and Jenna and her to put on.

Unfortunately, Mr. Hartley wasn't going to be home for another few days. He'd moved one family to Florida, where he then had to pick up another family and move them all the way to Seattle. He was working very hard because when the workers at the moving company he worked for went on strike a few months before, Mr. Hartley had joined them and had lost two months' worth of wages. Sometimes, big jobs took him away from home for a week. Other times, one or two days. Sophie didn't dare complain.

Still, it was disappointing.

It was Saturday, and the only company she had was a baby sister who was taking a nap and an older sister who was right there in the kitchen, ironing, of all the horrible things. Even John, whom Sophie could usually count on for company, didn't have time for her. His friend Tyler was over. When Sophie offered to let them play horses, Tyler grabbed John by the neck of his T-shirt and yelled, "Quick! It's the enemy!" and they'd run screaming from the kitchen. They were upstairs now, playing army, diving behind pillows and falling off the bed, pretending to be dead.

Thinking about the fun Jenna and Alice were having without her was bad enough. Being rejected by two six-year-old boys was the final blow.

"This is the most horrible weekend of my whole life," she said mournfully.

"You can always come shopping with me," said Mrs. Hartley.

Luckily, Thad chose that moment to come barreling down the stairs with a basketball under his arm and head for the back door.

"Have you cleaned your room?" Mrs. Hartley said.

"Not yet." He made a quick detour over to the table and grabbed a handful of cookies. "I'll do it later," he said as he disappeared into the mudroom.

"You'd better," Mrs. Hartley called after him.

"No fair!" said Sophie. "How come Thad's allowed to clean his room whenever he wants and we aren't?"

"Because Mom has one standard for Thad and another one for you and me." Nora buttoned the top button of the blouse she'd finished ironing and hung it beside her other clothes. "Don't you know that by now?"

"I do not," said Mrs. Hartley.

"You do, too," said Nora. "If Thad's in a bad mood, you get upset. But if Sophie or I am, you tell us to stop sulking. Thad *never* strips his bed. He always says 'Not yet,' and you let him get away with it. It's called a double standard."

"That's absolutely ridiculous." Mrs. Hartley closed the refrigerator door so firmly that the jars on the shelves rattled.

Sophie didn't usually compare herself to Thad; he was six years older than she was. But she was glad to see that Nora's superior tone annoyed her mother as much as it did her, and she was feeling ornery enough that the idea of ganging up on her mother made her feel better.

"Nora's right," she said. "When Thad borrowed a pair of Dad's underwear because he'd stuffed *his* dirty underwear under his bed, and then wrote his girlfriend's name on the elastic, all you did was laugh. But when I drew a picture of a horse on the wall over my bed, you got mad."

Actually, they had all laughed the night Mr.

Hartley pulled the elastic band of his boxer shorts above his belt at dinner to show them the words "Jaime Jaime Jaime," written on it with little hearts in between.

"It's not at all the same thing," her mother said testily.

Nora raised her eyebrows and pressed her lips together. She didn't say the word "transparent"; she *looked* it. For once, it wasn't directed at Sophie. She was delighted.

Mrs. Hartley was not.

"I saw that, Nora!" she said. "Oh, for heaven's sake! . . . Thad!" When his good-natured face appeared in the mudroom door, Mrs. Hartley said, "Go back upstairs and strip your bed this minute! I will *not* have my daughters accusing me of being a male chauvinist pig!"

"Aw, Ma," said Thad, "I've got a game."

"Now." His mother pointed toward the stairs.

"Thanks a lot, Nora." Thad made a lunge for her on his way back through the kitchen, but Nora was too quick. She held the ironing board in front of her like a shield. Thad smacked it with his hand.

"If I'm late, you're going to suffer!" He pounded back up the stairs, shaking his hand in pain.

"I'm getting sick and tired of having to argue about this every Saturday!" Mrs. Hartley said, banging pots and pans around on the stove as she spoke. "You're a bunch of lazy children is what you are! I work all week and when I ask for a bit of help, all I get is guff! You know I've been working more hours since Dad's strike. I have a good mind to turn *all* of the housekeeping over to you and see how you like it."

Her mother never stayed angry for long. Sophie knew the best thing to do would be to disappear and wait for it to blow over. But Nora and she hadn't agreed on anything in so long, and they certainly hadn't acted as a team. Sophie wanted to stick around to see what miracle might happen next.

There was a sudden blast of loud music as Thad opened his bedroom door and yelled down, "Which ones are the sheets?"

"Good grief," said Mrs. Hartley. She shot a quick look at Nora and Sophie as if *daring* them to say a word, and went out into the hall.

"What did I tell you?" said Nora, giving Sophie her look.

"Am I expected to believe that that is a serious question?" their mother yelled.

"I don't know which ones they are," Thad declared.

Nora rolled her eyes.

"For heaven's sake, Thad," said Mrs. Hartley. "The sheets! They're the things you sleep on! You're fifteen years old! I can't believe what I'm hearing!"

"Aw, man . . ." Thad disappeared back into his room again.

"The pillowcase, too!" their mother shouted.

Thad was in for it now, thought Sophie with delight. Their mother would *have* to agree with her and Nora. Maybe she'd make Thad change all the beds in the house for a few weeks, for practice.

But when Mrs. Hartley came back into the kitchen, it was clear she wasn't the least bit annoyed. If anything, she was amused.

" 'Which ones are the sheets' . . ." she said to herself, and laughed.

"You wouldn't laugh if *we* asked you that question," Sophie said.

"Oh, Sophie, stop," her mother said mildly. It was obvious that Thad had put her in a good mood, which made Sophie even grumpier. "I'm sick and tired of you both," her mother went on. "Go find something to do before I find something for you."

Nora wiggled her eyebrows at Sophie behind their mother's back, picked up her clothes, and left. Sophie knew better than to argue, so she got up and went into the family room. The Hartley children weren't allowed to watch TV in the middle of the day, so she flung herself on the couch and crossed her arms tightly across her chest.

It was no fair. Even when Thad asked dumb

questions, he got away with it. And how *did* Nora do that thing with her face?

Sophie got up and went into the downstairs bathroom to practice in front of the mirror. She wiggled her eyebrows and pushed her mouth into different shapes, but no matter how many different combinations she tried, she only managed to look as if she'd stepped into something soft and squishy.

Barefoot.

She had been at it for a matter of minutes when Thad came thundering back down the stairs. The lid of the washing machine banged, and Thad yelled, "I'm out of here!"

"Did you do it?" called Mrs. Hartley.

"Yep!"

"Be home by five!"

The back door slammed.

Sophie was immediately suspicious. She couldn't change her bed that fast, even when she didn't change it. She bet Thad hadn't touched his pillowcase.

She marched down the hall to the laundry room to investigate and found that her mother was already there. Mrs. Hartley held Thad's mattress pad in one hand and his blanket in the other. His sheets and plaid bedspread were piled up on the washing machine, with his pillow—still in its rumpled case—sitting on top.

"I knew it!" Sophie cried. "He cheated!"

She waited for her mother to explode, which Mrs. Hartley promptly did. She burst out laughing and stood looking from one piece of Thad's bedding to the other, shaking her head. "'Which ones are the sheets?'" she said, and chuckled.

To Sophie, it was the final straw.

She was still brooding about it when her mother made her take out the garbage after dinner and she saw that the lid of the garbage can wasn't on tight. She left it. It wasn't her job, Sophie decided; it was Thad's. Their mother never should have let him spend the night at his friend's house after what he did. He could put it back on the right way in the morning if he was so wonderful.

Trouble was, the raccoons got there first.

CHAPTER TWO

None of them were up yet when Mrs. Hartley came downstairs the next morning and discovered garbage strewn all over the backyard.

If they had been, they would have heard the back door slam and seen Mrs. Hartley jabbing at the buttons on the phone as she called Thad and told him to come home. If they'd seen her next, as she sat down at the kitchen table and started scribbling furiously on a large piece of paper, muttering to herself and occasionally laughing, they might have gotten a bit nervous.

The first Nora and Sophie knew that anything was going on was when Mrs. Hartley came upstairs and opened their door.

"Family meeting," she said. "Kitchen. Five

minutes. John, too." Very terse and deadly calm, as if something horrible had happened.

Or at least, that's the way it sounded to Sophie, who was already awake. It *had* to be horrible for her mother to call a family meeting at seven thirty on a Sunday morning; even Nora didn't grumble as they went across the hall to get John.

They filed into the kitchen just as Thad came in through the back door. He went over to the sink to wash his hands.

"Pee-euw," said John, pinching his nostrils together as he climbed up on the phone book on his chair at the kitchen table. "I smell garbage."

"What you smell, John," said Mrs. Hartley, in a voice that struck Sophie as eerily polite, "are old shrimp shells mixed with several-day-old chicken bones, some very-over-the-hill hamburger meat, and milk from the liners of Maura's bottles. Oh, and there must have been quite a few disposable diapers scattered around, too. Right, Thad?"

"With poop?" John said hopefully.

Thad's look darkened as he wiped his hands on his pants and sat down. "Thanks a lot, Sophie," he said out of the corner of his mouth.

"What'd she do?" said Nora.

"Left the top off the garbage can." Thad aimed a kick at Sophie's shin under the table for emphasis.

Sophie pushed her chair back in the nick of time. "It was *your* job," she said.

She checked over her shoulder to see if her mother was watching before she dared to kick Thad back. But Mrs. Hartley was acting strangely uninterested in them. She was pouring herself a mug of coffee and humming.

"Yeah, but I let *you* (kick, miss) do it, and you blew it," said Thad.

"*Let* me do it?" (Another kick.)

"You just couldn't handle it."

"Handle it?" More than anything, Sophie wanted to wipe the smirk off Thad's face. "In case you didn't know, I did it on purpose."

"Did you hear that, Mom?" said Thad, raising his voice. He and Sophie went on waging their silent kicking match and rocking the table back and forth. It wasn't nearly as much fun as it usually was, because Mrs. Hartley totally ignored them. She was buttering a piece of toast as slowly and carefully as if she were creating a piece of artwork.

"For heaven's sakes, Mom," Nora said at last. "Would you please yell at them and get it over with? Some of us would like to go back to bed."

"Oh, I think we're all a little tired of my yelling, don't you?" Mrs. Hartley said in a bright, false voice as she turned around. She picked up her mug and her plate and came toward them, smiling cheerfully as she put them on the table along with a large piece of paper. "I know *I* am," she added with a hearty laugh as she sat down.

Something was very fishy. Sophie didn't like it one bit.

"After all," their mother went on, "it doesn't work, does it? I just say the same things over and over again until I'm sick of the sound of my own voice. No one pays any attention!" She looked at them encouragingly. "Admit it.

You're sick of hearing it, too, you poor dears."

Sophie was a little put off by this strange performance. She couldn't remember her mother ever calling them "dears" before; it made them sound soft and cuddly, like bunny rabbits. But since her mother seemed to be heading in the right direction and Sophie wanted to encourage her, she said, "It's not so bad if we cover our ears. Thad's lucky. He uses his headphones."

"*Sophie*," Thad and Nora said together. "Shut *up*."

When her mother laughed her hearty laugh again instead of getting mad at them for saying shut up, Sophie really became uneasy. Something was definitely going on.

"Well, no one will have to suffer anymore," said the fake Mrs. Hartley. "From now on, everyone will know exactly what they have to do, and when, without my having to say a word."

Then she turned over the piece of paper and dropped her bombshell: It was a carefully executed job list, complete with everyone's name and what looked like a hundred jobs, all neatly laid out in boxes and rows. She would continue to do the laundry and the cooking, she informed them, but the rest of the household jobs would be divided up among them, so everyone would get to help.

"It's so much better that way, don't you think?" she asked gaily.

Sophie was torn between being glad everyone else was going to have to work and being appalled to see how many jobs they had to do, so she couldn't think of an immediate answer.

Mrs. Hartley didn't seem to need one. Unload dishwasher . . . mop kitchen floor . . . vacuum living room . . . clean downstairs bathroom—the jobs would rotate on a weekly basis beginning next Saturday, she explained, so that "everyone will get to do everything!"

She made it sound as though they were choosing which rides they wanted to go on at a theme park. John was the only one young enough to be deceived.

"What about me?" he said. "I want jobs, too."

"Downstairs bathroom?" Thad shook his head. "I don't do toilets."

"If girls can do toilets, so can boys," said Sophie. She stopped and thought about exactly what a toilet was. "I don't do toilets, either," she declared.

"Really, Mom," Nora said in a reasonable voice. "Don't you think you're going a little bit overboard here? These are all *your* jobs."

"That was a good one, Nora," Thad said later. The three of them had retreated to the family room. "Rubbing it in to Mom about the fact that she does all the work around the house." He stretched out on the La-Z-Boy and put his arms behind his head. "That was really sweet."

"Don't talk to me about sweet." Nora hurled a pillow that narrowly missed his head. "*You're* the one who got us into this."

"I didn't do it, Sophie did."

"I did not."

"Don't start that again," Nora said.

"John hardly has to do anything," complained Sophie. She plunked down at one end of the couch. "Collecting insects isn't a *job*. He loves insects."

Nora pulled her legs up under her in a neat lotus position at the other end. "Do you want to pick up spiders?" she said primly. "I don't."

Mrs. Hartley had made John his own list. He was already wandering around the house with a small box, looking for insects. Dead or alive, spiders mostly, brought in on Mrs. Hartley's flowers. He was going to let the live ones go outside, he told them, and coat the dead ones in clear nail polish and add them to his collection.

He was acting as though the whole thing was a game, and kept running back to the kitchen to read his name on the new "Hartley Family Job List" taped to the side of the refrigerator.

"And what about Maura?" said Sophie. "She doesn't have to do anything."

"You're really stretching it, Soph," said Thad.

"Well, it's true," Sophie said, kicking at the frame of the couch. "I don't know why

Mom didn't just yell the way she usually does."

"Maybe she's getting smarter," Nora said.

"Not a chance," said Thad. "Take my word for it: By next weekend, this'll be a thing of the past."

"It'd better be," said Sophie.

She was still smarting from Alice's phone call the night before. It turned out that Alice's mother had taken Alice and Jenna to the mall, where a new nail spa was offering nail polishing for only five dollars as part of its grand opening. It was a good thing there were only two of them, Alice told Sophie, or Mrs. Ireland wouldn't have treated them.

"It wasn't such a good thing for me," Sophie said in an injured voice.

"I didn't mean it that way," Alice said quickly. "It would have been much more fun if you were there. Really."

Sophie sniffed. "Treated you to what?"

"We both got our nails polished." Alice couldn't keep the excitement out of her voice. "It was so cool."

"Jenna did?" Sophie was shocked. The Jenna she knew, who wore her older brothers' cast-off high-tops and football jerseys to school? Who terrorized the boys on the playground when they played tag by bending their thumbs back, the way her brothers had taught her? "But she's a tomboy!"

"Not anymore," said Alice. "Her grandmother's here for a month. She said she'd take Jenna to Disney World if she starts acting more like a girl."

Jenna's nails were red with white stars, Alice reported breathlessly, and her own were purple—until she went out into the sun. Then they became pale pink with sparkles.

Sophie had stared glumly at her bitten nails the whole time Alice talked. It seemed to her Alice wasn't trying very hard to hide the excitement in her voice when she told Sophie every tiny detail, and she only said *twice* that she wished Sophie could have been there.

"It was so much fun," said Alice. "We decided to take turns coming up with special things to do on Saturday from now on."

"Who's 'we'?"

"Jenna and me. Jenna's turn is next Saturday. You have the Saturday after that."

It felt like an order; Sophie didn't like it. She didn't like it that Alice and Jenna had made up a new rule without asking her, either. It made their friendship feel lopsided. Like a three-legged table minus a leg.

She had to hang up on Alice to get her to stop talking. But not before she made Alice *promise* she and Jenna wouldn't go anywhere without Sophie next Saturday. One Saturday without her, and they were already making new rules. And now this, Sophie thought gloomily, turning her attention back to Nora and Thad.

"I don't know if you're right," Nora was saying. "Mom seemed pretty determined."

"What Mom seemed was demented," Thad said firmly. "This has to blow over. As I said: I don't do toilets."

Unfortunately, Mrs. Hartley was as good as her word.

Not only did she *not* change her mind, but she convinced Mr. Hartley to go along with her. They had a long talk in their bedroom on Wednesday afternoon when he got home. Sophie put her ear to their door to try and hear what they were saying, but she couldn't understand any of it. She thought her mother must have hypnotized him, though, because when they all sat down to dinner, her dad started talking in the same fake voice Mrs. Hartley had been using.

"I think a job list is a fantastic idea," he said jovially. "From now on, everyone will know exactly what they have to do without your mother or me having to say a word."

"Mom made you say that," said Sophie, "except you're supposed to also say 'and when.'"

"Good thing you're home, Dad," said Thad. "You can teach us everything you know about cleaning toilets."

"Hey! Wait a minute!" Sophie jumped up and went over to the refrigerator to confirm her worst suspicions. "Dad's name isn't even *on* the list!" she said, turning back around. "Neither is Mom's!"

Her parents laughed their extremely hearty laughs at this, which made Sophie even more indignant.

"You're like Ma and Pa in *Little House on the Prairie*," she said as she sat down. "Laura and Mary had to do all of the work around the house, too."

"It wouldn't be so bad, cleaning the outhouse," said Thad. "We could just toss in an old magazine every week for toilet paper."

Mr. Hartley seemed to find the whole thing hilarious. He was usually quiet and tired when he got home, but tonight he was having a fine time. "You know, honey," he said to Mrs. Hartley, "I think I'm going to think of a few jobs of my own to add to the chart."

"Good idea," she said in her fake voice.

"Like what?" said Nora. "'Watch TV' and 'read newspaper'?"

When Mr. Hartley didn't get mad at Nora for being rude, Sophie was even more convinced that her mother had done something to his brain. "Yep," he said, patting his stom-ach as he leaned back in his chair. "I'm look-ing forward to spending a lot more quality time with my hammock from now on."

He and Mrs. Hartley laughed their dumb laughs again.

Sophie was beginning to think it was much safer when her parents were mad than when they were happy.

Chapter Three

On Saturday morning, Sophie lay in bed with her fingertips pressed against her eyelids until white spots started whirling around in front of her pupils. She was sure it had to be very late by now. She opened her eyes and looked at the clock. It was only seven thirty-four: four minutes later than the last time she'd checked.

She sighed and got out of bed. She was going to have to come up with another way to waste time until Nora woke up. She certainly wasn't going downstairs to face her mother and the Hartley Family Job List alone.

Nora's feathery new scarf was hanging on the back of Nora's chair. Sophie wound it around her neck and made kissy faces at herself in the mirror, whipping the ends of the scarf back and forth like a movie star. She put Nora's sparkly hair band in her hair and threw more kisses to her adoring audience. Then she eased open Nora's underwear drawer—checking over her shoulder to make sure Nora was asleep—to look at Nora's bras.

She liked seeing them; they were so funny looking. The first time Nora brought one home, Sophie told her it looked like two egg cups held together by elastic, and asked if she could try it out with real eggs. Remembering how mad at her Nora had gotten made Sophie nervous. She quickly closed the drawer and looked around for something less dangerous to distract her. She spotted the perfect solution on top of Nora's dresser: nail polish remover.

Sophie unscrewed the cap and sniffed the bottle cautiously. Nora could hardly get angry at her for *smelling* her awake, now, could she? Besides, Sophie needed to use the remover. She sat down on the end of her bed and brought her knee up to her chin so she could reach her toes.

She'd complained bitterly to her mother when she missed having her nails polished with Alice and Jenna, and, at first, had got little sympathy.

"Nail polish on a nine-year-old-girl's nails?" Mrs. Hartley said. "And paying good money for it, too! What's next? Tattoo parlors?"

"Oh, Mom, *could* I?"

Ever since she'd seen the tattoo on the hip of the girl at the checkout counter at the grocery store, Sophie had wanted a tattoo more than anything in the world. Every time the girl reached forward to grab another item from the conveyor belt, a tiny kitten with a ball of yarn in its paws had peeked out at Sophie from its secret spot above the line of the girl's underwear, like a wink.

"I'll never ask to get my nails polished ever again," she said, clasping her hands together. "I *promise*."

"Honestly, Sophie," Mrs. Hartley said, laughing. "Sometimes I don't know where you came from."

"I'll get it on my bottom so no one will see..."

"Sophie!"

Sophie had sagged back against the cushions. She should have known. She'd listened to enough arguments between her mother and Nora over the years to realize that there were some things her mother was totally unreasonable about. The age at which girls were allowed to do certain things was one of them. Sophie knew them by heart: Nail polish to school at ten. Ears pierced at twelve. Makeup at fourteen, dates at sixteen, and "whatever you do, don't get married until you're thirty!" were Mrs. Hartley's iron-clad rules.

Many nights up in their bedroom, Nora had called their mother a "dinosaur." Sophie finally understood what she meant. Her mother was *never* going to let her do anything fun, she thought mournfully. When it was time to plan something special for *her* Saturday, all she'd be allowed to do was invite Jenna and Alice over for cleaning lessons.

"Oh, for heaven's sake. It's not the end of the world," her mother had said, patting Sophie's knee. "If you want to polish your toenails, go right ahead. You can use whatever polish you can find in my bathroom." And then, so grumpily that Sophie had hurried out of the room before she could change her mind, Mrs. Hartley added: "I can't remember when I *last* had the time to polish my nails."

It had to have been before Maura was born. All Sophie could find were a few nearly-empty bottles with caps that were almost impossible to open and brushes that were clumped together at the ends. Since there didn't seem to be enough of any one color, Sophie had ended up covering her toenails with thick dark pink, pale pink, and green—from the time when Mrs. Hartley had dressed up for a grownup Halloween party—dabs like polka dots.

When Sophie went downstairs to show her nails off, Nora laughed at her, but John liked them, so Sophie did his. Before she could decide whether she was going to show hers to Jenna and Alice, the dots had started to chip.

By Monday morning, it looked as if Sophie had been chewing her toenails as well as her fingernails.

It wasn't the same thing as going to a real nail polish store in the mall, anyway, she thought resignedly as she finished with her left foot and started on her right. The minute Sophie had seen Jenna's and Alice's nails at school on Monday, she'd decided to keep her socks on.

Their nails were very fancy.

For days, Jenna went around waving her hands in the air with her fingers spread apart so everyone could see them, and once Sophie caught Alice showing *her* nails to Destiny and Heather, two snobs whom Alice and Sophie and Jenna had pledged to ignore.

Sophie was glad when Alice came to school on Thursday with normal nails. She said her father had gotten tired of the stiff way she insisted on holding her fork at dinner to protect them, the way Jenna's grandmother had taught her. He made her take the polish off.

Sophie's stomach had started making grumbling noises. She wiped the polish off her last toe. Then she waved the dirty cotton ball in the air above Nora's head a few times and finally gave up the idea of smelling Nora awake. She could sleep for two more hours, easily.

Thinking it was still early enough for her to grab something to eat and make it back upstairs without getting caught, Sophie opened their door and stuck her head into the hall to listen for sounds of life.

The door to her parents' bedroom was closed. So was Maura's. Sophie tiptoed down the stairs—determinedly shielding her eyes from the sight of John in front of the television in the family room—and into the kitchen.

It was empty.

The path to the back door was clear.

Sophie was seized by a whiff of freedom so strong, she abandoned all thoughts of food and went straight to the mudroom. She didn't stop to think what Jenna's mother would say when she showed up on their doorstep at eight o'clock in the morning in her pajamas. All she knew was that she'd be free.

She carried her sneakers back to the kitchen and sat down to put them on. She was picturing herself on her bike, coasting down the hill to Jenna's house with her hair flying out behind her and the whole beautiful day in front of her, when she heard footsteps coming rapidly down the hall.

"There you are!" her mother said cheerfully as she sailed into the kitchen with Maura's diaper bag over one shoulder. "I was wondering how long you'd hold out!"

If Mrs. Hartley had seen the look on Sophie's face, she might have been offended. But she didn't. She didn't even look at Sophie. She was too busy bustling around the kitchen: opening drawers and pulling out plastic bags, pouring little crackers into one and cutting up grapes for another. The whole time she worked, she smiled to herself and hummed.

It was an annoying, tuneless hum. Sophie covered her ears and hummed louder to drown it out. From time to time, she took her hands away to see whether her mother had stopped. But Mrs. Hartley kept humming.

It was horrible to be in a bad mood and have the person responsible for it acting so happy. Sophie was sure her mother was doing it on purpose. She narrowed her eyes and directed sharp glances like little darts at her mother's back, hoping she would turn around. Her mother didn't seem to feel it. When Mrs. Hartley had finished packing everything into the diaper bag and added a bottle from the refrigerator, she stood in front of Sophie and flapped her hands for Sophie to take her hands away from her ears and listen.

"I'll get out of your way, so you can get going," she said when she had Sophie's full attention. "Thad's coming straight home from soccer practice, and I told Nora she needs to be up by ten. When everyone's here, you can tell John to turn off the TV, and the four of you can clean, clean, clean!"

She made it sound exciting, as though they were going to have a party, complete with music and food. Sophie frowned.

"If you have plans with Alice and Jenna, you

might want to get started on your jobs now," her mother suggested helpfully.

Sophie crossed her arms over her chest. "I'm not starting until everyone else does."

"Have it your own way."

Her mother left the kitchen as quickly as she had arrived, humming again as she hurried down the hall. Sophie kicked the leg of her chair and thought dark thoughts until Mrs. Hartley reappeared in the kitchen door, holding Maura.

"Wave bye-bye, Maura," she said, pumping Maura's little arm up and down.

"Sope! Sope!" Maura cried. She squirmed to get out of her mother's arms, leaning out for Sophie to take her, but Sophie was too cross to respond even to Maura.

The minute her mother's car crunched slowly past the kitchen window and disappeared, Sophie jumped up to call Jenna.

"Okay," Jenna said when Sophie said they shouldn't go anywhere without her, "but my mother said we're leaving *exactly* at twelve o'clock."

"Where're we going?"

"Remember the rule? It's a surprise."

"Who says it's a rule?" muttered Sophie, not liking the bossy tone of Jenna's voice.

"What?"

"Nothing. You'd better not leave without me." Sophie hung up the phone and sat back down to sulk.

Sulking isn't any fun when there's no one around to see it, so after a while she relaxed her face so she could get her cereal spoon in her mouth, and again a few minutes later to eat a doughnut.

It was very hard to sit glowering in an empty room with the television blaring, so Sophie stomped down the hall to tell John to turn it down. She didn't feel her face muscles sagging back to normal as she sat there watching, but the minute she heard Thad coming in the back door, Sophie hardened them up again and went to meet him.

"Two-zero!" he shouted when he saw her coming. "Two saves for Thaddeus Hartley! The man's a *MONSTER!*" He hurled his sweaty jersey at Sophie's head and headed into the kitchen. "Let's get this cleaning over!" he yelled. "I've got *plans!*"

"Pee-euw," said Sophie. She held his jersey away from her body fastidiously as she trailed behind him. "You have B.O."

Thad had finished scanning the job list and whirled around to face her. "Come on, Soph!" he shouted. "It's you and me!"

"We have to wake up Nora."

"There's no time!" Thad leapt into the air and planted an imaginary dunk shot in the sink. "Living room first! Sophie, it's your day to vacuum! I dust! Let's get going!"

He made it sound so exciting that Sophie's dark mood vanished. Their family fun time was finally going to start! She wheeled the vacuum cleaner down the hall and into the living room at top speed. Thad was bending over the coffee table. He looked up at her and winked.

"Watch this," he said. He drew in a huge

breath and directed a sharp blast of air at the surface of the table. A shower of dust and crumbs flew into the air.

"Hey!" cried Sophie. "It went all over the rug!"

"Then you'd better get vacuuming," said Thad. He did the same thing to the two end tables on either side of the couch and all of the lampshades. Each time he blew on them, the cloud of dust that swirled up into the air started settling back down almost immediately.

"They're going to be dusty again in about two minutes," said Sophie.

"Then whoever has 'dust living room' next week will have a job to do, won't they?" Thad gave her a friendly punch on the shoulder. "Dust happens, right, Soph?"

"Right."

"Come on, partner!" Thad spun around and bolted from the room. "Job number *two*, coming up!"

Thad was like a magician. Sophie was dazzled. He hardly ever paid attention to her anymore, and now she was his partner! She was suddenly glad Nora was asleep.

By the time she caught up with him, Thad was standing in the mudroom surveying the tangle of shoes, boots, sports equipment, and clothing that littered the floor.

"They ought to call it 'the mess room,'" he said. He jabbed her lightly in the side as he raised his voice. "Hey, John!" he shouted.

John came running.

Ever since Thad had showed him how to lift weights in the garage, John had been willing to do anything Thad asked. Mr. Hartley had started calling them "Little Pec" and "Big Pec" because of the way they kept showing off their muscles after every workout.

"I'll give you a dime to line up all these shoes and a nickel to do something about the clothes," Thad told John.

John squatted down and started arranging shoes.

"What about me?" Sophie protested. "I thought I was your partner."

"The one and only, Soph." Thad made a few quick passes over the floor with a broom and nodded toward the back door. "Get that for me?"

Sophie ran to open it.

"Whose job is 'sweep back porch' this week?" he said, with the broom poised to shoot a small pile of dirt out the door.

"Nora's."

"Perfect."

The next stop was Thad's bedroom. As she stood next to him in the doorway, Sophie could hardly wait to see how Thad was going to get out of cleaning *this*. It was a mess. Books were piled in precarious-looking towers on every surface, the wadded-up socks under the bed were covered with dust, and the pieces of the old computer Thad was taking apart were scattered all over the floor. It looked like a junkyard.

Even Thad was stumped, Sophie could tell. He stood looking at it for a few moments with his hand on the doorknob, plotting. Finally, he turned to her, and in a somber voice, said, "Like most things in life, little sister, cleaning is simply a question of mind over matter. *THINK CLEAN!*" he bellowed at his room, and shut the door.

Sophie stood stunned with admiration as Thad headed for the stairs. By the time she caught up with him in the kitchen, he had checked off every job under his name except for one.

". . . and last, but not least," he intoned, "Ye Olde Downstairs Bathroom. No problem."

"You said you don't do toilets," said Sophie.

"That depends on what you mean by the word 'do.'" Thad halted in the bathroom door and gave the room a quick glance. "Okay," he said with a curt nod. He took a deep breath, ducked inside, and turned on the tap in the sink. He immediately turned it off again, stepped back out into the hall, and let out his breath in a burst. "That was a close one," he panted.

"That's it?" asked Sophie.

"Looks good to me."

"What about the toilet? You're supposed to use the toilet brush with soap."

"Okay . . . okay . . ." Thad took another breath and leaned into the room again, peering cautiously into the toilet as though expecting to find a live crocodile swimming in the bowl. Then he ducked back out into the hall, breathed hard for a few seconds, and said, "You thought you had me stumped, didn't you?"

Sophie smiled.

Another sharp intake of his breath, a dive into the cabinet for the bottle, a few squirts of liquid soap, and Thad was back, breathing heavily, but alive.

"That about does it," he said.

"What about the brush?"

"This toilet doesn't need a brush—it's bald. Get it?" Thad ruffled her hair, said, "Tell Mom I'll be home at five," and was gone.

It was the most wonderful performance Sophie had ever seen. She stood there, reliving every amazing thing Thad had done. It was only after she heard the back door slam that she realized she hadn't done any of her own jobs yet.

It didn't faze her for a minute.

She ran to get her tiara and went back to the living room. The vacuum cleaner was exactly where she'd left it. Sophie settled the tiara firmly on her head and stood up tall.

"I hereby declare you *CLEAN!*" she commanded the room in her most regal voice.

Behind her, her mother said, "Good try, Sophie, but not quite."

When Sophie found her mother fast asleep on the couch after dinner, sitting up with her glasses on her nose and her book open on her lap, she was seized with a brilliant inspiration. Quietly, so as not to wake her, she sat down and put her mouth up to her mother's ear.

"No ... more ... family ... job ... list," she whispered in what she hoped was a soothing hypnotist's voice. She leaned forward and looked into her mother's face.

Nothing.

"No . . . more . . . family . . . *job* . . . list," she whispered, more insistently this time.

"No more dinners if you go on tickling my ear like that," her mother said in a normal voice without opening her eyes. She reached up and rubbed her ear.

"No fair," said Sophie. She sagged against her mother's side. "Don't you even feel a little hypnotized?"

"Not one bit." Her mother laughed and put her arm around Sophie's shoulders. "But I'll give you credit for not giving up easily."

"I'm still mad at you," Sophie said, trying to hold on to the indignation she'd felt this afternoon when her mother had refused to listen about Thad and made Sophie do all of her jobs. Mrs. Hartley had even double-checked to see how well she'd done them. Sophie hadn't finished until one o'clock. To make matters worse, Thad came home at five o'clock after having lost his basketball game and seemed to have completely forgotten that he and Sophie were partners in crime. He locked his bedroom door when she tried to come in and turned up his music, full blast.

Try as she might, Sophie could feel her anger oozing out of her as her mother ran her fingers slowly through Sophie's curls, gently untangling the knots Sophie always got from lack of brushing. It was peaceful sitting there, just the two of them: Maura and John were in bed, Nora was spending the night at a friend's, and Thad would be at a party until eleven o'clock.

"You are the master of your fate, you are the captain of your soul," her mother said. She always quoted from that poem whenever she wanted to tell them they were in charge of their own lives.

"I don't want to be the captain," Sophie said grumpily. "I bet Jenna and Alice did something really fun again."

"Maybe they got facelifts!" Mrs. Hartley said brightly. "After all, they're nine."

"Ha-ha, Mom."

Her mother swept Sophie's hair away from her forehead and gave her a light kiss right above her scowl line. "How about if you go make some popcorn while I go up and wash my face and get into my bathrobe," she said, smiling. "You and I can actually watch a movie *we* want to see without having to negotiate with the boys."

"Can I pick it?" said Sophie, sitting forward.

"Sure. But nothing with guns and fast cars."

"Okay. And nothing with policemen."

Sophie ran into the kitchen and scrambled up onto the counter. She wasn't even going to point out to her mother that making popcorn wasn't on the job list, she thought happily as she opened the cupboard. *That's* how good she suddenly felt.

CHAPTER FOUR

Sophie saw the rest of the class lining up at the door to the cafeteria, which meant she wasn't going to get to finish telling her story about Thad. Not that Alice and Jenna seemed all that interested.

She probably shouldn't have started with the toilet.

Alice, who was an only child and thought that having an older brother was romantic, giggled and said, "Thad's so cute." But Jenna knew how disgusting brothers could be and was totally unimpressed.

"*Eeuuw*," she said, with a fussy little shake of her head, "who wants to talk about toilets?" and started describing their visit to the beauty parlor on Saturday with her grandmother instead. She kept saying, "Right, Alice?" and "Remember?" as if Sophie needed to be reminded that she hadn't been there.

It was all they talked about for the rest of lunch. "My hair was as hard as a rock," reported Alice.

"I thought it looked beautiful." Jenna shook her head so that the tiny braids covering it rattled their beaded ends together. She'd been doing that all morning. Sophie was sick of it.

"You looked at least eleven," said Jenna.

"My mom said I looked forty-five." Alice, who was wearing her normal ponytail, had looked resigned. "And my father said I reminded him of his great-aunt who went bald and had to wear a wig made out of horsehair."

"Oh, really!" Jenna gave another rattle. "My grandmother said we both looked very feminine."

"Feminine?" said Sophie. She frowned. The word made her feel vaguely embarrassed, as though it was one of those "personal" things they weren't supposed to talk about until they were older. "What's that supposed to mean?"

"You know." Jenna shrugged. "Looking like a girl."

"What else is Alice supposed to look like? She *is* a girl."

"My grandmother said it's good to be feminine," said Jenna.

"You don't even *like* your grandmother," said Sophie. "You said she's bossy. You like your grandfather better. He takes you to baseball games."

"My grandfather died last year, in case you didn't know," Jenna said with an injured rattle of her beads.

"Too bad," Sophie said feelingly.

"You two—don't fight," said Alice. She looked at Sophie with a wave of red already moving up over her face and said, "I think it means . . . you know . . . ladylike." Alice lifted up her shoulders as if she was trying to hide her scarlet face and added, "Kind of . . . *soft* inside."

Sophie was horrified. Alice's face looked the same way Nora and her friends' faces looked when they huddled on the beds in her and Nora's room during a sleepover and talked: embarrassed and excited at the same time.

Nora always pushed Sophie out of the room before she could hear what they were talking about, saying, "Sorry, but you're too *young* for girl talk," and shut the door firmly in her face.

Sophie was just as glad. She thought girl talk was silly. And now her two best friends were doing it.

"I'm sick of talking about hair," she said. "It's boring."

"That's only because you weren't there," said Jenna.

"Jenna, that's mean," said Alice.

"Sorry, Sophie." Jenna tilted her head to one side and stuck out her lower lip to make it look as if she was sincere. But Sophie knew she just wanted to feel the beads against her cheek.

"We missed you," Jenna said.

Sophie stuffed her half-eaten sandwich into her lunch bag and stood up. "You are so *transparent*," she said.

"So?"

It was totally deflating. Sophie wished she'd thought of it herself.

"Three forks, three knives, three spoons?" asked Mr. Hartley as he sat down at the dinner table. He held up the large soup ladle that had been lying next to his knife. "What kind of feast are we having?"

"I ran out of regular spoons," said John, who was now stacking napkins in neat piles beside each place setting.

"John, I told you not to do that," said Mrs. Hartley, peering at him through the steam rising from the pot she was stirring.

"It's John's week to set the table," Nora explained to their father. She finished pouring milk into a row of glasses on the counter and began ferrying them over to the table. "Thad helped him come up with a plan so he only has to set it once."

It wasn't such a bad idea, Sophie realized as she banged the plate of bread and butter on the table. She could see every plate, glass, and bowl in the house, stacked in piles that would dwindle as the week went on.

"If John gets to do it, so do I," she said.

"John!" said Mrs. Hartley.

"Dummy," John muttered to Sophie, picking everything back up. "Big fat *dummy.*"

"Don't go upstairs empty-handed!" Mrs. Hartley called from the family room after dinner. She did that automatically when she heard someone heading for the stairs, the same way she called, "Lift the seat!" when she heard someone go into the downstairs bathroom. Or "Turn off your lights!" when they all came charging down the stairs for dinner.

Sophie looked at the piles of assorted belongings Mrs. Hartley regularly collected from around the house and left on the stairs for people to carry up to their rooms. "None of it's mine!" she shouted.

There was a thunderous silence from the family room.

Sophie grabbed a pile and continued up the stairs. "Don't *you* come up empty-handed, either," she said crossly when she heard some-one start up behind her.

She turned around just in time to flatten herself against the wall as Thad barreled past her carrying his saxophone case. "Sorry, my hands are full!" he called cheerfully as he disappeared down the hall.

"You could carry something under your *arm!*" shouted Sophie. Then, "No fair!" when she heard his door slam.

So *that's* why Thad gave up the violin for the saxophone. He said it was because he wanted to play in the school's jazz band, but now Sophie knew it was really so that he'd have something big to carry and wouldn't have to bother with their mother's piles.

Fine, she thought mutinously. From now on, *she* was going to start carrying something big of her own. Maybe she'd take piano lessons and really show Thad. She could hardly be expected to carry a pile when she was carrying a whole piano, now, could she?

She was brooding her way down the hall to her room when she heard somebody on the stairs and ran back to supervise. John was halfway up, leaning against the wall for balance and taking one careful step at a time, a bucket of Legos in each hand.

"No fair!" wailed Sophie, and promptly dropped her pile in protest.

"Who left this mess in the hall?" Mr. Hartley said in a loud voice some time later.

"Not me," Nora said, her head in her homework.

"I did," Sophie called. She put down her horses and hurried into the hall. "I forgot," she muttered. She could feel her father's eyes on her back as she scuttled around like a crab on the floor at his feet, collecting things. Only after he moved off down the hall did she feel bold enough to add, "It's not even on the list."

By the next morning, it was.

"Why don't you get a cleaning lady? They do everything," Jenna said as the three of them walked into school.

"I don't know about *everything*," said Alice.

"My mother cleans our house before the cleaning lady comes."

"Okay, but all you have to do is make your bed, right?"

Alice nodded. "Really, Sophie," she said earnestly. "Tell your mother to get one."

"I don't think she wants one," said Sophie.

"How can she not want one?" asked Jenna. "Everybody does."

Sophie thought about all the times her mother had said, "Do I look like a *cleaning lady* to you?" when she reminded them to pick up after themselves. She didn't make it sound very respectable. And the one time Thad joked, "As a matter of fact, Ma, you kind of do," Mrs. Hartley got mad at him.

"I'm almost positive my mother doesn't," Sophie said.

"Maybe it's because she never had one," Alice said helpfully. "If she had one, I bet she'd like it."

"It can't hurt to ask," said Jenna.

But of course it did.

———

"Are you joking?" Nora said scornfully when Sophie brought it up in their bedroom after school. Sophie was changing her clothes to go outside and ride her bike. Nora had put her books and notebooks on her desk in neat piles in preparation for doing homework. Ever since Thad had started taking AP classes in high school, she'd been working harder than ever, trying to keep up.

"Mom and Dad can't afford a cleaning lady," she said. "Why do you think they're working more hours?"

"Because we're poor?" said Sophie, immediately feeling that they were.

"Don't be such a baby. They don't have a lot of extra money, that's all." Nora whipped her hair back into a ponytail as if it had done something to offend her, and sat down. "Stop worrying and go away. I have to do my homework before chorus practice tonight."

But Sophie couldn't stop worrying. She brought the subject up again at dinner.

"I wouldn't have a cleaning lady even if we

could afford it, which we can't," her mother said comfortably. She passed a plate piled high with chicken to Nora on her right, while deftly taking a bowl of carrots from Thad on her left. She had made Mr. Hartley remove the lazy Susan from the middle of the table after the night John and Thad had started spinning it like a roulette wheel and sent a bowl of beets flying onto the floor. Now they were supposed to practice saying polite things like "Please pass the bread" and "May I have the carrots?" during dinner.

"Please don't pass the carrots," John said loudly when she was about to serve him some. "I hate cooked carrots."

"Your father and I believe that helping out around the house builds character," Mrs. Hartley went on, putting a small pile of carrots on John's plate. "Why do you think we had five healthy children? Well, only four can help right now," she said, with a fond smile at Maura in her highchair.

"If you didn't have so many children, maybe

we could afford a cleaning lady," said Nora.

"And you'd all be spoiled rotten," said Mrs. Hartley.

"I could live with that," said Thad.

"I think a person should be a certain age before they get a cleaning lady, don't you, Mom?" Sophie said encouragingly.

"Yeah, right, Sophie." Nora rolled her eyes. "For you, it's one hundred. For me, it's thirteen."

"Enough of this silly talk," said Mrs. Hartley. She looked around the table. "Whose week is it to set the table? I don't see salt and pepper."

The dumb old job list, Sophie thought glumly as John went to get the salt and pepper from beside the stove. It always came back to that.

"What'd she say?" Jenna asked as they filed down the hall to gym the next morning. "Are you getting one?"

"I don't think so," Sophie said.

"Why not?" said Alice.

"My mother thinks a person should be fifty before they get a cleaning lady."

"Fifty?" Jenna stopped walking. "What kind of rule is that?"

"You know Sophie's mother," said Alice. "She's very strict."

"She says helping around the house builds character," said Sophie. "She doesn't want us to be spoiled rotten."

Jenna put her hands on her hips. "Are you saying Alice and me are spoiled rotten?"

Sophie was thinking how she could answer without insulting Jenna to her face when Alice came to her rescue.

"Not Sophie—her mother," Alice explained patiently. "It's because she's a nurse. Right, Sophie?"

"Right." Sophie wasn't sure what the connection was between being a nurse and being strict, and she didn't care. Thanks to Alice and her mother, she'd finally been able to say what she'd wanted to say to Jenna for days.

She tilted her head to one side and smiled. "Sorry, Jenna," she said.

Nora would have seen right through her.

"You should see him!" Sophie said to Nora indignantly. "He's out there whipping around, having fun and drinking soda out of a can, and Mom says it's a job. But we're not allowed to do it! And she's letting him do it during the week, too, so he can play soccer on the weekend, but the rest of us have to waste our entire Saturday morning doing *our* jobs!"

The job list had been up for more than a week. Tempers had become so frayed that Sophie and Nora got into a huge argument on Saturday about exactly what *time* the jobs changed for the week, and each tried to make the other one mop the kitchen floor. Mrs. Hartley had made them both do it: mop it, as well as wax it, which took *hours*. Sophie had had to call Jenna and Alice and say she couldn't have her Saturday.

Mr. Hartley had looked positively relieved when he headed out the door for his next moving job. He had added "cut grass" to the list before he left, stating that the person had to be fifteen in order to use the mower. That meant Thad was the only one who could do it, and Thad *loved* driving the riding mower. He pretended it was a car and drove like a wild person, careening around the back and front yards and swerving around bushes and trees as though he was on an obstacle course. He said he was practicing for getting his license.

"So what's new?" Nora said unsympathetically. She was on her hands and knees scrubbing the bathroom floor that everyone else was perfectly happy to leave dirty and was clearly in no mood to listen. Sophie felt very glad she didn't have Nora's high standards. It meant that now Nora had to clean the children's bathroom along with all of her other jobs, even when it wasn't her week.

"Honestly, Sophie, I don't know how you can put up with it like this." Nora sprayed a coat of foamy cleanser around the bathtub and attacked it with a brush. "There's hair everywhere! And look at this ring! How can you stand it?"

"I don't look at it."

"And what about the toilet?" said Nora. "It's absolutely foul!"

"Those yellow spots belong to Thad and John, and you know it," Sophie said with a little sniff. "*They* should clean it."

"Yes, but they don't!" said Nora. "And you're so lazy, you'd rather sit on them than clean them!"

Sophie decided that this would be a very good time to leave and continued down the hall, rubbing the seat of her pants and trying not to think about all the times she'd sat on those spots when they were still wet. Boys didn't care if the toilet seat had spots because they didn't have to sit down.

Or they did, but only half the time.

It wasn't fair, she thought as she went into her room: Boys got a much better deal than girls when it came to cleaning the house. Sophie was sick of it.

She'd noticed that her mother had stopped

opening Thad's door since she came up with the list. And that when she went into John's room and found his Legos scattered everywhere, she left them there because John told her, "I'm working on something."

Fine, Sophie thought defiantly. Then *I'm* thinking about wearing those again, she decided, looking at the shorts balled up on her chair. And I can't close the book that's lying face-down on the floor because I'm still thinking about reading it.

"If you don't want to think clean, then don't," she told her half of the room as she sat down on her bed. "And I *like* the dust on my bureau," she went on in a loud voice. "It keeps the WOOD WARM!"

"If anyone is losing their marbles around here, it should be me." Nora staggered into their room and flopped face-down on her bed with a groan. "With the cleaning fumes I've been breathing, it's a miracle I'm still alive."

"Nora, your spread!"

Nora rolled over sluggishly and stared up at the ceiling. "Oh, I know," she said, moving her legs to one side so that her feet hung out over the edge of the bed. "I'm getting tired of worrying about things being clean, that's all."

Sophie could hardly believe her ears.

"Have you noticed that all we ever talk about at dinner anymore is cleaning?" Nora went on in a dazed voice. "And I *like* cleaning."

As if Nora were an exotic bird that would fly off at the slightest movement, Sophie leaned toward her cautiously and said, "John and Thad have it much easier."

"That's because Thad's a lazy slob and John's not much more than a baby," said Nora.

"He has his own special list of easy things, like picking up sticks in the yard and bringing in the mail," agreed Sophie. "Maura could practically bring in the mail."

Nora rolled her head to one side to look at Sophie for a minute, and then rolled it back and stared up at the ceiling.

"Okay," Sophie said quickly. "But I still think it's no fair. Girls end up doing more than boys."

"It's called inequality," said Nora, "and it's because we're saps."

"*I'm* not a sap," Sophie protested.

"Thad got out of doing his jobs last weekend, but you missed another play date because we had to do the floor, remember?"

This wasn't the time to get annoyed with Nora for calling it a play date. Sophie looked at her in silence.

"You're a sap," confirmed Nora, closing her eyes.

"Well, I'm not going to be one from now on," Sophie said. "You know what I think?"

"What?"

Sophie was so shocked that Nora actually wanted to know what she thought, she almost forgot her idea entirely. Luckily, it had been growing in her mind for so long and been lovingly watered with such generous doses of indignation that it had firmly taken root.

Sophie was able to pick it now and hand it to her sister like the inspired gift she believed it was.

"I think we should go on strike."

CHAPTER FIVE

"On strike?" Mrs. Hartley repeated after dinner on Thursday.

Sophie glanced quickly at Nora, who raised her eyebrows and shrugged. "It was your idea," the eyebrows said. "Good luck," said the shoulders.

Sophie tried not to panic. The strike had been going on for two days, but so far no one had noticed. And now wasn't the best time for the subject to come up.

Their father had arrived home tired and grouchy from his trip. What little he had said at dinner was about the woman in the family he had just moved. She had stood over him and his crew, insisting that they wrap everything in three sheets of paper before they put it in a box.

Every single thing, he grumbled, down to a vegetable peeler and a three-quarters-empty plastic bottle of cooking oil. The packing bill was "astronomical."

"Money must grow on trees in some neighborhoods," said Mrs. Hartley.

"People are lazy." Mr. Hartley took a bite of his hamburger.

"Everything?" Sophie asked him. "Even toilet paper?"

"Right off the rollers in the bathrooms."

"Did you get any good jewelry?" said Nora, who had recently taken to wearing rings on all five fingers and bracelets on both wrists.

"Nora's going to be a jewel thief when she grows up," reported John. "I'm going to blow up the safes."

They went on trying to name things that their father couldn't possibly have had to wrap until Sophie finally said, "What about air?"

When her father admitted he hadn't packed

air, Thad showed off his high school status by saying, "What about a single proton? Or the nucleus of an atom? You couldn't pack that."

John finally got over-excited and named the most daring thing he could think of. "Even underwear?" he shouted, almost falling off his chair. "Even *dirty* underwear?"

"John," said Mrs. Hartley. "Eat your dinner." To the rest of the table she said, "Could we move on, please? You all have homework," so the conversation petered out.

After dinner, Thad went up to his room and Mrs. Hartley took John up to get his bath started while she put Maura to bed. Sophie and Nora were in the family room watching television when their father came in from cleaning the cab of his truck. He flopped into his recliner with a groan.

There was a loud crackling noise. Mr. Hartley jumped up again and lifted the cushion.

"Nice," he said. He held up a crumpled plastic container and a fork in the air. "Very nice. Whose job is it to clean the family room this week?"

Sophie's heart had started pounding the second she heard the noise. "Mine," she said meekly.

"For heaven's sake, Sophie." Her mother came briskly into the room and, in her typical way, figured out the situation at a glance. "Take those to the kitchen this minute." Her father held them out, clearly expecting her to leap up and do it.

Sophie didn't think she could even if she wanted. She seemed to be paralyzed.

So, of course, she had to tell her parents what was going on.

"Who's 'we'?" asked her mother in the stony silence that followed.

"Nora and me."

Mr. Hartley gave a snort that meant he didn't want to have anything more to do with the conversation, and put the crumpled plastic container and fork on the coffee table. He sat down and noisily unfolded the newspaper, holding it up around his face like a fence.

"Don't be ridiculous," said Mrs. Hartley. She sat down, too, and picked up the TV remote. The way she clicked it, to make it perfectly clear that as far as she was concerned the conversation was over, made Sophie become unparalyzed.

"It's not ridiculous," she said. "Nora and me are on strike."

It was hard work, keeping her eyes on her mother's during the silent stare that followed. Sophie had to remind herself about the book she'd read on dog training (in case her parents ever broke down and let her get a dog) to stop herself from looking away.

The important thing to remember, the book said, is that a dog is a pack animal. The leader of the pack is the dog that doesn't look away in a fight. If your dog did something bad, you had to stare it in the eye until it looked down. The dog that won the staring contest was the boss.

Mrs. Hartley could have taught the most stubborn bulldog a lesson or two. Just when Sophie's eyeballs felt as if they were about to pop out of her head and she was beginning to accept the fact that her mother would *always* be the leader of the pack, Mrs. Hartley flicked her eyes at Nora and then back to Sophie and said, "And what are you on strike *for?*"

Sophie felt a rush of triumph.

"Because Thad and John aren't doing as much work as we are," she said. "Thad does a horrible job with all the things on his list, and all John has to do are things he likes. They don't have to work as hard as Nora and me because they don't care how dirty the house is and we do."

"You *do?*"

"Nora does," Sophie replied staunchly. "It's not fair. We aren't going to do any of our jobs until the boys help more. Dad went on strike when he thought something was wrong, and so can we."

Behind his newspaper, Mr. Hartley snorted, and then coughed.

Their mother looked at Nora. "Do you have anything to add?"

"Not really," said Nora, "other than the fact

that I'm glad Sophie's finally becoming aware of a situation that's been going on for a long time."

She sounded so injured and dignified, it made Sophie feel bold.

"Boys are male pigs," she said to her mother. "You said so yourself."

"Nice." Mr. Hartley lowered his newspaper to look at his wife. "So that's the kind of language that goes on when I'm not here."

"For heaven's sake, Sophie!" said Mrs. Hartley. "If you're going to quote me, get it right! I didn't say they were male pigs! I said Nora was making me sound like a male chauvinist pig!"

"What's the difference?" asked Sophie.

Her mother opened her mouth to answer, and then shut it. Opened it again, and shut it, sighing a noisy sigh of defeat.

Mr. Hartley chuckled. "Kind of backed you into a corner there, didn't she?" he said to her sympathetically. Then he looked at Sophie and his face was stern. "Going on strike isn't fun, you know," he said. "It's hard work. People put their beliefs on the line. They don't do it on the spur of the moment and then change their minds when the going gets tough. You have to be sure of what it is you're striking for and not back down until you get it."

"I know," said Sophie. She hadn't really thought about it that way and was a bit worried by how serious he made it sound. What did he mean, "when the going gets tough"?

"There'll be repercussions," her father said. "You realize that."

Sophie hadn't realized that. She didn't even know what it meant.

"What kind?" she asked cautiously.

"I don't know." Her dad's voice was pleasant as he lifted up his paper again. "We'll just have to wait and see, won't we?"

"What's a repercussion?" Sophie whispered as she followed Nora up the stairs.

"How should I know? I'm not a dictionary," Nora said. "But it doesn't sound good, does it?"

"They'll probably just happen to Thad." Sophie spoke with more confidence than she felt. She was a bit worried that Nora was right, but she didn't want Nora to know that. Nora was already making noises about quitting.

When Sophie had first suggested it, Nora said it would never work. Sophie had been forced to launch into a lengthy description of the clumps of scum-coated hair that constantly clogged the bathtub drain, the piles of damp towels nobody ever hung up, and all of the times their mother had favored Thad, using point-by-point examples.

When in a desperate, last-ditch effort she finally compared Nora to Cinderella, she thought she might have gone too far. By that time, though, it was clear Nora *felt* like Cinderella. She'd reluctantly agreed to go along with Sophie's idea.

"What'd you *think* was going to happen?" Nora said now, opening the top drawer of her dresser and pulling out her nightgown. "That Mom was immediately going to side with us and make Thad work harder? That the strike would be over, just like that?"

Since that was pretty much what Sophie *had* hoped was going to happen, she was momentarily discouraged to realize she'd been wrong. Then she remembered what her father had said, and took heart. When Nora left to go to the bathroom, Sophie stood in front of the mirror to give herself courage.

You're the Leader-of-the-Pack, she told herself, making a face. No, not that way. A little more frown, maybe. Maybe bare her teeth a bit . . . ? There. That was more like it.

"What's wrong with your teeth?" Nora said as she breezed back into the room.

"Nothing." Sophie turned to her. "Good things *are* going to happen," she said firmly. "We're putting our beliefs on the line, like Dad said."

"Let's just hope no one steps on them," said Nora.

Sophie told Alice and Jenna about it the next day.

"Nothing exciting like that ever happens at my house," Alice said enviously.

"What do you think your parents are going to do?" Jenna's eyes were huge.

"I don't know, but we're not backing down."

"Alice and me can come over and strike with you tomorrow," Jenna offered eagerly. "It's still your Saturday, anyway."

Sophie briefly considered the idea of using Jenna and Alice to form a picket line and marching back and forth outside the Hartleys' back door, holding placards and chanting. But then she imagined her mother's face and stopped.

"I'd better put off my Saturday until next week," she said.

"Again?" chorused Jenna and Alice.

"There are going to be repercussions around my house any minute," Sophie said ominously. She had repeated the word in her head enough times that she could say it with authority. "You don't want to be around when those happen."

"Cool." Jenna sounded so envious that Sophie immediately forgave her for having been so annoying over the past few weeks.

"Are repercussions bad?" asked Alice.

"Very bad," said Sophie.

"I'm an expert at repercussions because of my brothers," Jenna volunteered. "There's usually lots of yelling and door-slamming."

"Poor you, Sophie," said Alice.

"What do you mean?" said Jenna. "I wish *I* was on strike."

It was really very gratifying.

In truth, the effects of the strike on the Hartley household so far had been a disappointment. Sophie would have welcomed repercussions with open arms compared to the complete lack of interest anyone was showing.

True, small things started to happen, almost at once, but no one seemed to mind them very much. The jobs she and Nora had that week were the kind no one noticed hadn't been done. Or if they noticed, they didn't care.

When Mr. Hartley discovered the words "LAST DUSTED, 1789" written in the dust on the coffee table (it was Sophie's week to dust; she was sure Thad wrote it), all he did was laugh. And John was thrilled when he found a centipede crawling in the dirt on the mud-room floor while looking for his shoes. (It was Nora's week to sweep.) He promptly put it in a glass jar with waxed paper over the top and took it to school.

It was Sophie's job to carry up Mrs. Hartley's piles. After several days, they reached almost to the top of the stairs; she was sure someone was going to object. But when Thad tripped over one as they were hurrying down to dinner one night, all he did was yell, "So *that's* where my soccer shirt is!" and pull it out from the bottom of the pile.

The next day, Sophie found John sitting on a pile halfway up the stairs. He was playing with his dinosaurs.

"Don't you think these piles are dangerous?" she said.

"I like them dangerous." John bashed the T-Rex against the Stegosaurus a few times and yelled with satisfaction as the T-Rex tumbled down head over heels and landed at the bottom.

"Maybe you should tell Mom," Sophie said encouragingly.

"What do you think I am?" said John. "A *girl*?"

Sophie tried to make her stories as exciting as possible when she reported back to Alice and Jenna, but she was getting discouraged. What was the point of going on strike if nobody noticed? What if their house just got dirtier and dirtier and no one cared except Nora?

Nora was going to quit. Sophie was sure of it. She was already showing signs of weakening. Sophie had caught her wearing flip-flops into the bathroom so her feet wouldn't have to touch the floor. She'd had to start spying to make sure Nora didn't clean and ruin everything. She was on her knees in the hall one night, peering through the keyhole while Nora brushed her teeth, when Nora suddenly opened the bathroom door and caught her.

"You don't want to be a strikebreaker, do you?" said Sophie, following Nora back to their room. "I was trying to protect you."

It wasn't until Tuesday night, after Mrs. Hartley put John and Maura to bed and came back down to join the rest of them watching TV, that Sophie thought something was finally going to happen.

Just as she was about to sit down, her mother discovered an open bag of potato chips wedged between two cushions, and crumbs scattered all over the couch. She looked so annoyed, Sophie felt a glimmer of hope. Her mother wouldn't be able to ignore the strike now, she was sure of it. She heard her mother draw in a sharp breath, and waited for the explosion.

There wasn't one. Sophie's face fell as Mrs. Hartley curved her mouth into her fake smile. With a dramatic gesture like a movie actress, she grandly swept the crumbs onto the rug and sat down.

"Chips, anyone?" she cried with her horrible false cheerfulness. "Tom? A chip?" she said, holding the bag out to Mr. Hartley.

"Don't mind if I do," he said. He took a whole handful. "Sure beats having to go into the kitchen and open a cupboard to find them."

Sophie wasn't the only one who thought her parents sounded crazy.

"What's going on?" said Thad, looking from their mother to their father with a puzzled look on his face. "You two feeling okay?"

"Never better," said Mrs. Hartley. She beamed first at him, and then at Sophie and Nora, in turn. "Whose clever idea *was* it to leave the bag here so conveniently?"

"John was eating them before dinner," Nora told her in a frosty voice. "For heaven's sake, Mom, calm down."

"Chips before dinner!" their mother cried. "What a wonderful idea!"

Nora wouldn't even *look* at Sophie when they went up and got ready for bed, and when Sophie said she thought their mother was finally "cracking," Nora made a rude noise through her nose and snapped off the light.

Sophie lay awake in the dark, staring up at the ceiling. It was very hard, being the organizer of a strike. Her father said that all the workers in his strike had banded together. The way it looked now, Sophie worried she was about to become a band of one.

She tossed and turned, finally getting herself so tangled up in her sheets that she had to get out of bed and unwind her nightgown from around her neck before she strangled herself. Then she got back into bed again and sighed.

If anyone was about to crack, it was Nora. Sophie couldn't blame her. It was certainly beginning to look as if nothing was going to happen.

Then Thad found out what they were doing, and things did.

CHAPTER SIX

The kitchen smelled.

Not of good things, like cakes baking and onions frying, but of garbage. Sophie sat down at the table to do her math homework after school, anyway. Doing it upstairs would have been giving in.

Sophie always did her homework in the kitchen. Usually, her mother was cooking dinner or making herself a cup of tea after work. Sophie was glad to have her around in case she needed help. She often asked her mother questions she already knew the answer to just so they could talk.

Talking to her mother made her feel good.

Today, though, Sophie was relieved that Mrs. Hartley had dropped her off and gone to pick up John; it would have been impossible for Sophie to sit there pretending. She was breathing through her mouth and hurrying to finish her homework so she could go and sit in a better-smelling room when someone came in through the back door.

It was Thad. Sophie heard him whistling as he hurled his backpack and books on the bench in the mudroom. She hunched over her paper and scribbled like mad so Thad would see how hard she was working and go straight upstairs without noticing the smell.

Or talking to her. She especially didn't want him to stop and talk to her.

"Holy cow," Thad said as he came through the door. "What stinks?"

Sophie peered up through her hair as Thad gave a few experimental sniffs. He yanked open the door under the sink and promptly shut it again. "Whose week is it to empty the garbage?" he asked.

Sophie looked back down at her paper.

"I don't know why you haven't passed out," he said sympathetically. He walked over to the refrigerator and ran his finger down the list. Then his voice changed. "Sophie!" he said. "It's *your* week! Get that thing out of here!"

"What thing?" Sophie asked, looking up with wide eyes.

Thad took a step closer. "Is that *cotton?*" he asked incredulously.

At first, all Sophie could pull out were wispy threads. She panicked, thinking she was about to shove the cotton balls she'd stuffed into her nose all the way up to her brain. Then she got a good hold on them and yanked them out.

"You are such a weirdo," Thad said admiringly.

Sophie shoved the soggy balls into her pocket and stood up. She picked up her book, her paper, and her pencil, and announced as haughtily as she could, "I'm going someplace *quiet* so I can *con*centrate."

"Whoa, whoa, whoa, whoa, whooooooa." Thad slipped around in front of her to block her escape route and pointed back over her shoulder. "Sophie," he said, "empty the garbage."

"I can't."

"Sure, you can," Thad said patiently. "You open the door . . . you take out the garbage can . . ."

"We're on strike."

That stopped Thad cold.

"You are?"

Sophie nodded. She tried to give Thad her Leader-of-the-Pack stare, but with her nose crinkling as the horrible smell wafted up around them, she felt more like a pug than a Great Dane.

Luckily, Thad couldn't stand the smell, either, because he suddenly said, "Wait a minute," and yanked open the door under the sink again. He pulled out the garbage can and ran outside to dump it into one of the large cans next to the back porch.

In the meantime, Sophie took out the spray that was supposed to make a room smell like a field of wildflowers and sprayed it lavishly around the kitchen. She aimed a shot toward the ceiling and lifted her face to it, imagining she was walking through a mist as the drops tingled against her skin.

The mist smelled better than the kitchen, but not by much.

"That's enough!" Thad yelled as he came back into the room. He grabbed the can away from her. "What're you trying to do, kill us?"

Sophie sat down and crossed her arms over her chest, prepared to resist Thad's interrogation. The room smelled both sweet and rotten. She didn't see how they would be able to ignore it when they sat down for dinner.

"Who's 'we'?" asked Thad, sitting down across from her.

He sounded so interested, Sophie was torn.

Nora had said they shouldn't tell Thad about the strike because he was every bit as much the enemy as their parents. She'd also said that Thad wouldn't notice that anything was different, anyway, because he was such a slob.

She'd been right about that part, Sophie had to admit. But she liked Thad. The trouble with thinking of him as the enemy was that it meant practically everyone in the family was the enemy.

Sophie was getting lonely.

"Come on, Soph," he said. "What's up?"

Sophie knew she shouldn't tell him; she knew it would end badly. But if she didn't talk to somebody, she was going to burst. She could always tell Nora that Thad had tortured her. With room freshener.

It had made her dizzy and she'd told him everything.

"Nora and me," she said.

"No kidding." Thad whistled. "Do Mom and Dad know?"

Sophie nodded.

"What'd they say?"

"Nothing."

"Nothing?" Thad sat back. "Since when do Mom and Dad say nothing?"

"Since we went on strike."

Her parents hadn't said much of *anything* to her since she'd told them about it, Sophie realized glumly. Her father had gone out on the road again two days later, and her mother was so tired and grumpy, Sophie had been steering clear of her.

She even missed her mother's fake laugh.

"What do you mean, you're on strike?" Thad said. "I haven't noticed anything."

"We stopped doing our jobs."

"Nora, too?"

Sophie nodded.

"You mean to tell me, she stopped scrubbing our bathroom floor?"

Another nod.

"No cleaning the grout with a toothbrush?"

Sophie looked back at him, mute.

"Wow." Thad was clearly impressed. "You two must really be mad about something. What're you protesting?"

Sophie sighed. She wished their friendly conversation didn't have to turn ugly. "You," she said.

"Me?" Thad didn't sound mad, he sounded amazed.

"John, too."

"Holy cow. What'd we do?"

"Nothing."

"Sophie," Thad said reasonably, "you're not making sense here."

"Yes, she is. She just does a lousy job of explaining." Nora staggered into the room and dumped a huge pile of books on the kitchen table. "What did I say about not telling?" she said to Sophie.

"She didn't have to tell me, Nora," said Thad. "In case you haven't noticed, it stinks in here."

"Fake wildflowers," Nora said with a professional sniff, "and rotting meat. You two are so lame." She went over to the sink and threw open the window above it, then switched on the fan over the stove. "How can you sit there and not do anything about it?"

"We didn't just sit here—" Sophie began, but Thad held up his hand to silence her.

"You explain it if you're so superior," he said to Nora. "What'd John and I do?"

"Nothing. Just like Sophie said." Nora had taken out a bottle of ammonia and was pouring it into a shallow bowl, which she plunked down in the middle of the table. "Mom made a big deal of coming up with a Hartley Family Job List to make things equal, and *you* continue to do nothing."

"What do you mean?" Thad protested. "Who mows the lawn? Who drags the garbage cans out to the sidewalk?"

"You love mowing the lawn," Nora pointed out. "And the garbage cans are too heavy for us."

"Yeah, well, getting down on my hands and knees and scrubbing the bathroom floor is too menial for me," said Thad.

"Menial?" Nora said, bristling.

"What does 'menial' mean?" asked Sophie, looking from one to the other.

Thad ignored her. "You're nuts, the way you clean everything all the time," he said. "Why should John and I have to suffer?"

"*Suffer?*" Nora's voice went up an octave. "I'm cleaning *your* lousy hairs and dirt, and hanging up *your* wet towels so we won't all die from mildew inhalation, and *you're* suffering?"

"If it means it hurts your knees, it's too menial for me, too," Sophie declared.

"The more I think about it, the more unfair it is." Thad stood up and pushed in his chair. "I'm going on strike, too."

"Only you would go on strike against yourself," said Nora.

"You can't have two strikes in one family," Sophie said firmly, vainly hoping they'd listen to her for a change. Neither of them even looked at her. They were too busy glaring at each other.

"I'm not striking against myself," replied Thad. "I'm striking against you."

"Me?" Nora snorted. "*You* have a nerve."

"For inflicting cruel and unusual cleanliness on John and me."

"You are so lame."

The whole thing was falling apart in front of Sophie's very eyes. What had started out as a battle over principles had deteriorated into a family squabble. Sophie was sick of it.

"*You! Can't! Have! Two! Strikes! In! One! Family!*" she shouted.

Thad and Nora were momentarily stunned. Then Nora covered her ears and yelled, "Stop it!" and Thad said, "What do you think you're doing, Sophie?" and snatched away the large spoon she'd been banging against a pot to emphasize each word.

"I am trying to get a word in edgewise," Sophie said in a dignified voice. "There can only be one strike in a family at a time. If you want to go on strike, Thad, you have to join ours."

"Sophie! Whose side are you on?" Nora said. "*He's* the one we're striking against!"

"He's only half of what we're striking against," Sophie said. "Mom and Dad are the bigger half. If the kids don't stick together, we'll never win."

"Halves are the same size, you dope," Nora said impatiently.

"Sophie's right." Thad slung his arm over Sophie's shoulder and hugged her against his side so hard, she could hardly breathe. "I'm joining *you*, but not her," he said, jerking his head at Nora.

"Thad, don't." Sophie squirmed out from under his embrace. This was one time when she didn't want to be his partner. "We want to get rid of the job list, don't we?" she said pleadingly to Nora.

"I'd rather get rid of Thad."

"Ditto to you," said Thad. He held his hand up for Sophie to slap. "All for one, one for all, right, Soph?"

"Good going, Sophie," Nora said, after Sophie had reluctantly made her traitorous gesture and Thad had gone thundering up the stairs. "Just don't ask me for any more advice, okay?" Nora banged the last book on the top of her considerable pile and started slowly out of the room.

"At least now, maybe something will happen!" Sophie called.

Nora didn't bother to answer.

"Something has to happen sometime, doesn't it?" Sophie asked the empty room wistfully.

The faint smell of garbage reassured her that it probably did.

CHAPTER SEVEN

"Whose week is it to set the table?" called Mrs. Hartley.

Sophie tightened her grip on Maura's hands. Maura had been staggering around the family room for what felt like hours, listing from side to side like a sailor on a tossing ship. Sophie's back ached from the effort of bending over.

She would gladly have gone on suffering for the rest of the night rather than face her mother in the kitchen. Technically, it was her week. She'd been able to avoid a confrontation so far because on Sunday night they had a barbecue and ate off paper plates. Sophie had defiantly left hers on the picnic table, but Thad crumpled them all up and practiced sinking shots with them in the garbage can.

Then last night, Mrs. Hartley had to go to a meeting and left Thad in charge. They all ate pizza right out of the box. Their mother would have had a fit.

"Sophie!"

"I think Maura's about to walk by herself!" shouted Sophie, stalling. She held her breath in the silence that followed.

"Come set the table!"

Sophie sighed and dumped Maura abruptly in her playpen. When Maura opened up her mouth to cry, Sophie quickly handed her a rubber giraffe to chew on.

"We're having hot dogs and baked beans," her mother said when Sophie came into the kitchen. "You don't have to bother with knives."

Mrs. Hartley was moving quickly between the stove, the sink, and the toaster oven. She didn't turn around. "Be sure to put ketchup and relish on the table. Oh, and mustard. And call Nora to pour the milk, would you?

It's her week. And tell John to wash his hands."

Sophie didn't move.

"What're you waiting for?" her mother asked, sounding slightly annoyed as she turned around. "Dinner's ready."

"I can't," said Sophie.

"Why not?"

Her mother's eyes had the wild, distracted look they got when she had too much to do and was about to say, "All I need is another pair of hands."

Watching her made Sophie feel guilty. It was one thing for them to go on strike against their parents. Ganging up against their mother felt a little mean. Sophie would have loved to jump in and help her.

"The strike, remember?" she said.

"Oh, for heaven's sake."

Her mother had completely forgotten, Sophie could tell. For a split second, Sophie wished she could forget, too. That they all could, just for tonight. They could sit around the table and eat dinner like a happy family, the way they used to.

Then her mother drew the battle line in the sand again.

"I've had about as much of your silly little strike as I can take," she said.

Sophie's back stiffened. "It's not silly," she said.

Her mother stared at her for a minute without speaking, then turned and yanked open the cupboard door. She began pulling out dishes and crashing them on top of one another in a way she would have yelled at any of the children for doing. "Fine," she said tersely. "We'll have a do-it-yourself dinner, then. Go call the others."

The meal ended up being more of a free-for-all than a do-it-yourself.

Thad made Nora mad by spearing three hot dogs to put on one roll. John insisted on pouring his own milk, dribbling half of it on the counter in the process. He insisted on helping himself to potato chips, too, and managed to dump almost the entire bag on his plate before Sophie could grab it from him. Chips flew all over the floor.

She quickly got down on her hands and knees to gather them up, sneaking glances up at her mother to see if she had noticed.

Her mother ignored it.

Her mother ignored all of them, except for Maura, during the entire meal. She gave short, choppy answers when anyone talked to her and didn't comment when Thad put his elbows on the table or when John blew bubbles in his milk with a straw.

It was obvious that Thad had told John about the strike. John kept putting his hands over his mouth and jiggling his shoulders up and down to show how funny he thought it was. When their mother got up to get something from the refrigerator, Nora hissed to Thad, "For heaven's sake, *do* something about him, would you?"

Thad bopped John lightly on the head with his fork.

It was a very short dinner.

Mrs. Hartley finally lifted Maura out of her

high chair and went over to the sink for a wash-cloth. "Dishwasher?" Thad mouthed silently, looking around the table.

Nora tapped her chest grimly.

"Don't do it!" John jumped up and jabbed his fork in the air like a sword. "We're on str—" Thad clamped his hand over John's mouth before he could finish and swept him, struggling, out of the kitchen.

Sophie looked at the dirty plates on the table and then at Nora.

"Go," Nora mouthed.

As Sophie came down the hall, John was marching back and forth in front of his bedroom with a long stick resting on his shoulder like a rifle, chanting. "Strike, strike, strike, strike. Strike, strike, strike, strike."

"You don't even know what you're striking for," said Sophie, thinking it might be nice if she were six again and the strike was all a game.

"For fun," said John.

She sat on her bed and played with her horses for a while. She combed out their tails and manes and made whinnying sounds, but her heart wasn't in it. She couldn't stop thinking about Nora and wondering what she was doing about the dirty dishes.

She couldn't leave them on the table. Their mother would have a fit. But if she put them in the dishwasher, she'd be breaking the strike. It was only a matter of time before the garbage started to smell again, too, Sophie realized gloomily, and it was getting harder and harder to find a place to sit in the family room that wasn't covered with something.

How could her mother go on sitting with them through dinners like the one tonight? And when he got home, what would their father do? What if their parents stopped eating with them altogether and they became one of those families where everyone ate standing up, whenever they wanted?

Sophie thought all of her worrying must have jarred something loose in her brain because she suddenly heard clinking noises. Then Nora came into their room carrying a large plastic bag with both hands. Without a word to Sophie, or even a look, she knelt on the floor and yanked up the dust ruffle on Sophie's bed.

"What're you doing?" Sophie asked.

Nora started cramming the bag under the bed. "You don't think I'm putting them under *my* bed, do you?" The job completed, Nora pulled the dust ruffle down again and stood up. "I did it this one time, but that's it. *You* can figure out what to do with them tomorrow."

Sophie fell asleep with a happy smile on her face. The smell of hot dogs and ketchup wafting up from under her bed was even better than perfume.

It was the proud smell of a united front.

"Paper plates?" Alice said the next day, sitting down at the table next to Sophie. "*Your* mother?"

"I put a stack of them on the kitchen counter this morning," Sophie reported. "Mom didn't say a word. Not even when John took his breakfast outside to eat on the porch, like a picnic."

"What's so bad about paper plates?" said Jenna. She sat down on Sophie's other side. "At my house, we eat right out of the bags sometimes."

"For Sophie's mother not to say anything is really bad," Alice said.

"Maybe she's as stubborn as Sophie," Jenna said.

Sophie got a horrible, sudden image of two bulldogs, nose to nose, growl to growl, neither one willing to give in. "I think she's ready to crack," she said quickly, blinking it away.

"Cool," said Jenna. "What're your demands going to be?"

"I don't like to think of them as 'demands,'" Sophie said cautiously, picturing the expressions on her parents' faces if she were to even say the word.

"That's what they're called," Jenna insisted. "You're not getting cold feet, are you?"

"Maybe you should call them requests," said Alice.

"Only *you* would call a demand a request, Alice," said Jenna.

"Well, you make *everything* sound like a demand, Jenna."

"What do you think a strike is about?" Jenna retorted.

"You don't know everything."

"No fighting." Sophie held out her arms like a referee at a boxing match as they leaned across her. "I have enough of that at home."

There was a stiff little silence from either side.

It felt wonderfully familiar. Sophie felt the three-legged table wobbling and knew exactly what to do.

"I think you should *demand* an apology from Jenna, Alice," she said, turning to her left, "and I think *you* should request Alice not to be so demanding," she said to Jenna.

They both thought Sophie was hilarious. They all sat around saying silly things for a while, just for the pleasure of laughing.

Lunch ended on a very cheerful note.

———

The sight of her father's truck in their driveway after school brought Sophie crashing back down to earth.

She rounded the corner of the house, and found Nora, Thad, and John waiting for her on the back porch. They were sitting in a disapproving row on the top step. "What's Dad doing home?" she asked, slowing to a crawl. "What's everybody looking at me for?"

"He lives here, remember?" said Nora.

"The jig's up, Soph." Thad flashed a quick smile.

"Yeah, you big troublemaker," John said.

Sophie's heart sank. "What happened?"

"John's insulted because Dad told him to go away when he knocked on their bedroom door," Nora told her.

"You didn't really think we could keep it up when Dad got home, did you?" said Thad.

"I don't see why not," Sophie said.

"Dad and paper plates?" Nora shook her head. "I don't think so."

"Nora's right." Thad stood up and walked around behind Sophie. He clamped his hands firmly on her shoulders to discourage any thoughts of escape, and began pushing her toward the house. "You've got to go in there and negotiate, Soph," he said encouragingly. "You can do it."

"Right. Knock 'em dead," Nora shifted to one side to let Sophie up the steps.

"Why me?" asked Sophie, looking around, in vain, for any signs of support.

"You're our one-and-only strike organizer," said Thad.

"Our one-and-only Little Miss Strike Authority," agreed Nora.

"You started it," said John.

"Oh, all right." Sophie reluctantly opened the door. "But what are our demands?"

"A Ferrari," said Thad as he settled down happily to wait. "Navy blue."

"The right to take a shower without wearing flip-flops," said Nora.

"Torpedoes," said John. "Tyler and me need more torpedoes."

———

"Ah, Sophie."

From the sound of her father's voice, Sophie could tell her parents had been expecting one of their children to show up; they just hadn't known which one. They sat side by side on the edge of their bed, smiling at her.

"What can we do for you?" said Mr. Hartley.

"I came to see if you're ready to negotiate," she said gruffly. She was wearing her Leader-of-the-Pack face.

"What's wrong with your teeth?" her mother asked.

"Nothing."

"Oh. Well, I don't think I'm ready to negotiate. Are you, dear?" Mrs. Hartley said, turning to her husband with a bright smile.

"Not me."

"Then not me, either."

They both smiled at Sophie again.

With their huge, expectant smiles, they reminded her of wolves. Sophie felt a queasy stirring in her stomach. As if a huge crater, like the ones she'd seen in photographs of earthquakes, was slowly opening up in the floor at her feet.

"You aren't?" she said.

"Not at all." Her mother beamed. "I've just been telling Dad what an *interesting* learning experience this has been. Haven't I, dear?" She patted Mr. Hartley's hand.

"I would say that Mom's eyes have been opened up in a most *educational* way," he agreed.

The chasm was growing wider. Sophie didn't dare look down. She was sure she'd see smoke rising out of it and a huge hand with warts on the knuckles reaching up to drag her in. "Like how?" she asked carefully.

"Well, you children know how hard Dad and I have been working lately," her mother began, "and I know you understand that certain things need to be done in order to keep a household running. After all," she said brightly, "except for Maura, none of you are babies anymore, are you?"

It was one of those questions that didn't require an answer. Sophie felt the cold finger of fear draw its line down her backbone.

"But what I *didn't* know," her mother went on, her brow furrowing suddenly, as if the part she was coming to saddened her, "was how much you don't know about *cooperation!* And *family.*" Her mother folded her hands in her lap. "I truly didn't understand how little my own children know about family. I can't tell you how instructive it's been."

There was a long silence in the room. Sophie was sure she could hear Nora and Thad and John breathing heavily at the bottom of the stairs. Since she was pretty sure the Ferrari, and the clean bathtub, and the torpedoes were out, she didn't look forward to going back down to face them.

"So," she said cautiously, trying to feel her way and having no idea of what to do next. "What are you going to do?"

Smiles cut her parents' faces in two. Sophie knew that her side was sunk.

"We're going on strike, too," said Mrs. Hartley.

CHAPTER EIGHT

Sophie didn't need an alarm clock to wake her up for school. The noisy sounds of life her family made in the morning were enough. The next morning, however, it was the silence that made her sit up.

Thad wasn't pounding on the bathroom door, yelling that Nora had been in there for too long. Mrs. Hartley wasn't calling up from downstairs that they were about to miss the bus. Nora wasn't even pulling out one dresser drawer and then another and complaining loudly about not having anything to wear.

She was still asleep under her covers.

Sophie looked at the clock.

"Nora!" she shouted, scrambling out of her bed. "Get up! We're late!" She shook Nora by the shoulders, making the whole bed shake. "It's almost seven!"

Sophie dragged a T-shirt over her head. Shoving first one leg into her jeans and then the other, she hopped around their room while Nora shrieked and ran into the bathroom. Sophie ran down the hall, banging on Thad's and John's door as she went, like a fireman alerting people to a fire in the house.

"Mom!" she called, pounding down the stairs. She ran into the kitchen and stopped. Her mother was peacefully reading the newspaper at the table with Maura in her highchair beside her. "Why didn't you wake us up?" Sophie asked accusingly.

Mrs. Hartley looked at Sophie and smiled. She lifted up her mug and took a sip of her coffee. She leaned over and wiped cereal off Maura's chin. Then casually, she said, "I don't believe that's my job anymore, is it?"

"That was so rotten," said Nora as they hurried down the back steps. "I cannot believe Mom would sink that low."

"They *are* on strike," said Thad, taking a bite of the dry, untoasted bagel he had grabbed. "Although it certainly was an eye opener."

Mrs. Hartley had laid out their demands to Sophie plainly and simply: She would continue to do the grocery shopping, since they all had to eat, but the children would be responsible for the cooking. They would fix their own lunches, too, and do the laundry.

"I'm sure you'll agree it's only fair, since Dad and I earn all the money," her mother said. "Of course, we'll continue to contribute our paychecks to the running of the house. Although we'd much rather take a trip, wouldn't we, dear?" she asked Mr. Hartley.

"I've always wanted to see Dublin," he said.

Sophie had been too shocked to protest, but she had been thinking about it all night. "She didn't say anything about not waking us up in the morning," she said now, bringing up the rear. "I don't think parents are even allowed to go on strike. I bet there's a rule against it."

"Show me the rule book," said Thad.

"She's really asking for it now," Nora said. "My hair's still damp. I didn't even have time to put on my makeup." She blinked a few times. "Well, I did have time to put on mascara, at least. But fine." She held out her arm with her hand curled into a fist. "She wants war. We make war, right? All for one, one for all!"

Sophie tapped her fist against Nora's and Thad's, astonished. Suddenly, they had become the Three Musketeers. They would have to let John in, she thought as Nora and Thad headed for their bus and she got into the car to wait for her mother and John. That would make it Four Musketeers.

But still. She was gratified by the change in Nora. In the back of her mind, though, wiggling like a worm in the grass, was the worry about how long they'd be able to hold out.

"I'm not touching it," Nora said. "*You* touch it."

"Why should I touch it?" said Thad. "I cooked dinner the last two nights."

"I thought they took the hair off," said Sophie.

The raw chicken their mother had brought for them to cook for dinner lay on the cutting board in front of them. It looked more like a baby than a chicken. A naked baby, without a head. And with little hairs sticking out of it.

Sophie wasn't crazy about the hairs.

"You only offered to cook so you could use the grill," said Nora. "Anyway, hot dogs are more like plastic than real meat."

"The hamburgers were real meat."

"They didn't look like cows, though, did they?" said Nora. "This looks like a dead chicken."

"With its hairs still on," added Sophie.

"Oh, Sophie, be quiet!" Nora ordered. "Chickens don't have hair, they have feathers. Please, Thad," she said, switching to her pleading voice. "You clean fish—"

"Fish don't have arms and legs," said Thad. "Call me when dinner's ready."

"Thad!" Nora cried. "Oh, I *hate* you!" She stamped her foot when the back door slammed and rounded furiously on the chicken as if she'd caught it trying to sneak away. "I'm *not* touching you, do you understand? You're disgusting!"

Sophie, who'd been rummaging around in the cabinet under the sink, called out in triumph, "It's all right! I can touch it!" She backed out, feet first, and held her hands up in the air like a surgeon preparing to operate. Their mother's yellow dishwashing gloves came up to her elbows.

Quickly, so she wouldn't feel the loose skin slipping around over the chicken's bones, she picked it up and dropped it into the pan. Nora opened the oven door.

"Aren't we going to put anything on it?" Sophie asked as Nora slid the pan inside and slammed the door shut.

"Like what, a blanket?"

"I think we were supposed to take out something from its stomach," Sophie said doubtfully. "Mom uses it to make gravy."

"Yes, well, Mom's not doing the cooking tonight, now, is she?" said Nora, furiously punching the buttons on the stove. "And if you think I'm reaching inside that . . . *thing's* . . . stomach, you're crazy." She untied the strings to her mother's apron and draped it over a chair. "The cookbook said to start it at five hundred degrees. Make sure you turn the oven down to three-fifty in fifteen minutes," she instructed as she picked up her purse and slipped her backpack over one shoulder. "And when the laundry's done, make sure you put my white blouse in the dryer. On low. I need it for my concert tomorrow."

Sophie trudged down the hall to the laundry room without complaining. It had only been two days, but everyone was getting grouchy. Thad had cooked for the first two nights, and Nora had done the laundry.

Today was Sophie's turn. Nora had given her strict instructions about separating the whites from the coloreds, but that sounded like twice as much work, so Sophie had ignored it and thrown everything in together. She was feeling like both the cook and the cleaning lady as she opened the lid of the washing machine and began pulling out clothes.

Heavy, wet, pink clothes.

The higher the pile got, the pinker it looked. Upon closer inspection, Sophie discovered that she'd dyed not only Thad's underwear pink but all of Nora's white things, as well. She panicked and threw all of the pink garments back into the machine. She poured in two capfuls of soap, plus a third for good measure, and shut the lid again.

That should do it, Sophie thought grimly. *I'm* going outside.

She rode her bike around the block a few times until Nora yelled out their bedroom window something about her blouse. Sophie went back inside and found the floor of the laundry room covered with soapy water.

A veritable tidal wave of it was heading straight for the rug in the hall.

Sophie grabbed the dry laundry that was in the basket waiting to be folded and used it to mop the water up. As soon as the potential disaster was over and she saw the pile of now-soggy clothing on the floor, she realized she was going to have to wash that pile again, after first rewashing the pink things in the machine to get the extra soap out.

"Sophie, stop it! You'll wake Maura!" her mother ordered from the doorway to the laundry room. She flapped her hands and looked unsympathetically at Sophie, who was sitting on the damp floor. "What *are* you wailing about?"

Sophie sniffed. Then she frowned and sniffed again. A fierce frown wrinkled her face as realization dawned.

"Nail polish?" she said, outraged. "You're putting on *nail polish* while I have to do the laundry and the cooking?"

The cooking.

The exact second Sophie remembered the chicken, the smoke alarm went off. She could hear people shouting in the kitchen above its piercing wail.

"Well, what'd you expect?" she growled unrepentantly when she arrived on her mother's heels to see Thad carrying the smoking pan with the burned chicken out onto the back porch. "I can't do all the work around here."

When John heard that the things they'd left inside were the chicken's heart, liver, and neck, he begged to be allowed to take them out and operate on them, but Mrs. Hartley made Thad throw everything away. They had peanut butter and jelly sandwiches for dinner, instead.

"I had peanut butter and jelly for breakfast, peanut butter and jelly for lunch, and peanut butter and jelly for dinner," John said happily, gazing around the table at the less cheerful-looking members of the family. "I could eat peanut butter and jelly for the rest of my life."

"At the rate we're going, you might have to," said Mr. Hartley.

"We need to talk." Nora slapped her pencil down on her desk and swiveled around in her chair to look at Sophie. They had retreated upstairs to their bedroom the minute dinner was over. Sophie was glad for an excuse to stop working on the math problems she was having no success with, and put her pencil down, too.

"Talk about what?" she asked.

"We just can't sit around waiting for one side to die of jelly poisoning," Nora said. "Thad! Come in here!"

"Our side would probably win," said Sophie. "I bet John's immune to jelly poisoning by now."

Thad came from down the hall and leaned against their doorjamb. "Strike meeting?" he asked expectantly.

"We have to do something," Nora said.

"Dad went out after dinner to find somewhere to watch TV that doesn't make him sneeze," Thad said. "He just came back."

He and Nora exchanged glances. "Time for another negotiation session, Sophie," they said at the same time.

"Not *again*," Sophie groaned.

Thad took her gently but firmly by the arm and pulled her to her feet. "They're in the family room," he instructed as he pushed her slowly into the hall. "You go down . . . you tell them you're worried we're all losing weight . . ."

"That'll get Mom, for sure," agreed Nora, who had put her hands in the middle of Sophie's back and was helping push. "Do whatever you have to. Yell. Beg. Cry. Try crying, Sophie. You're good at that. Just don't come back without a settlement."

They reached the top of the stairs.

"You're our fearless leader," said Thad, standing next to Nora as Sophie started reluctantly down. "We're with you all the way."

"Well, not *all* the way, obviously," Nora said in a low voice.

"I heard that, Nora!" Sophie called.

Deep in her heart, Sophie was glad. This time, she wouldn't back down, she thought as she walked along the hall. She would stick to her guns. Their parents were sick of this, too. They would negotiate calmly so life could go back to normal. They'd get rid of the family job list . . . their mother would start cooking again . . . and doing the laundry. . . . Sophie was so deep in thought as she walked into the family room that at first she didn't understand what she was seeing. And then she did.

Her father was about to chomp on the slice of pizza in his hand. Her mother was halfway out of her seat, reaching for the pizza box on the table in front of her. The expressions on both of their faces were as amazed as Sophie felt.

They looked like statues in a wax museum. The "Guilty Parents Caught in the Act" display.

The feeling of betrayal that flooded Sophie's heart knew no bounds.

"Pizza!" she cried. "You traitors!" and burst into tears.

CHAPTER NINE

". . . and half the time nobody would listen to me . . . and Nora and Thad are always competing with each other . . . and Thad's only nice to me when he wants something . . . he *uses* me!" Sophie wailed. "Even John was mean to me, and John's *never* mean. But that's not the worst thing," she went on. "We were putting our beliefs on the line, and you and Dad were *cheating!*"

Sophie took a deep, shuddering breath and paused. It felt wonderful to be sitting between her parents on the couch. It was as if a dam inside her had burst and all the worries and sorrows of the past few weeks were flowing out. Remembering how many there had been, and how things had ended up, she felt tears rising in her eyes again. Except now, she was more indignant than sad.

"Everybody in this family is selfish," she said. "Even you and Dad. It's not fair when you say we don't know about family, because you don't know about family, either. All you do is work, and then you come home tired and grumpy and get mad because the house is dirty."

"I have to work. We need the money," said Mrs. Hartley.

"But you like it, too," said Sophie.

"Yes, I do."

"You never *used* to care about everything being so clean," Sophie sniffed.

"I still don't," Mrs. Hartley said. "But you children expected me to do everything unless I nagged you. I got tired of it."

Sophie liked it better when her mother agreed with her. "Well, it still wasn't right to eat pizza behind our backs," she said.

"No, it wasn't. You're absolutely right."

Sophie had never had such a string of successes in her life. It was only because her parents were feeling sorry for her, she knew. They were feeling guilty, too. Sophie recognized a great opening when she saw one.

"You won't even let me get a tattoo," she said, burying her face in her mother's side and sounding as pitiful as she could.

"Faker!" Mr. Hartley shouted. He grabbed Sophie and tickled her in the stomach until she shrieked.

"Crisis is over!" he called. "You can come out now!"

Nora and Thad and John filed sheepishly into the room. They stood just inside the door, as if waiting to make sure it was really safe.

"Does anyone have anything to say in response to Sophie's comments?" Mrs. Hartley asked, sweeping her eyes over them severely, as though they were in a police line-up.

"Sorry, Sophie." John scooted across the room and burrowed down between Sophie and their mother.

"Who put the dirty dishes under your bed, Sophie?" Nora protested. "I did it for you, didn't I?"

"With a friend like that, you don't need enemies," said Mr. Hartley. He looked at Sophie and winked.

"Sophie's right," said Thad, nodding at the pizza. "That's pretty low."

"Help yourselves," said Mr. Hartley.

It was a tight fit, with all six of them on the couch. There was a friendly silence for a few minutes while they ate. Sophie sat squished between John on one side and Nora on the other. She sighed contentedly between bites.

"The only one missing is Maura," observed Mrs. Hartley.

"I don't want the strike to be over," said John. "I like going on strike."

"Too bad. It's over," said Sophie. "Our side says: No more Hartley Family Job List."

"Then we're back where we started," said Mrs. Hartley. "I don't want to go there, as you children would say."

"Any suggestions?" said Mr. Hartley.

"I don't know about the rest of you, but I like it better when the house is clean."

They all (except for John, who went on eating) looked at Thad in astonishment.

"What?" he protested, holding up his hands. "I do. It's easier to think. The family room was getting a little grotty, if you know what I mean. I'm talking foot smell here, people."

Thad cowered against the couch, covering his head with his hands for protection, as the girls and Mrs. Hartley pummeled him with pillows. John grabbed one of Thad's legs and pulled, shouting, "Leave him alone! Thad, run!"

"A bit hard to do on one leg, John," Mr. Hartley said. He had sat back and was watching the riotous scene from the sidelines.

Thad's attackers finally left him under a pile of pillows and fell back against the couch, laughing. "I never thought I'd live to see the day when Thad said he likes the house clean," Mrs. Hartley said breathlessly.

"I never thought I'd live to hear him say he thinks," said Nora.

There was a lot of good feeling in the room. No one seemed inclined to argue, so after a bit of discussion, they agreed to go back to the rules of everyone picking up after themselves, and pitching in when their mother asked.

"And Thad, if any dirty clothing is left around the house for more than twenty-four hours," Mrs. Hartley said, "I'm going to throw it out. You can pay to replace it."

"Why are you only looking at *me*?"

Mrs. Hartley wisely ignored him. "Nora," she went on, "I'm afraid you have got to accept the fact that you have a higher standard of cleanliness than your siblings. If you have to do more in your bathroom to raise it to your standards, so be it."

"I should have been born a slob like the rest of them," Nora said.

"Cooperation." The sound of Mr. Hartley's deep voice made everyone look at him in surprise. He usually left household cleaning discussions, along with every other kind of household discussion, up to Mrs. Hartley.

"That's what we're talking about here," he said when he had everyone's attention. "Pulling together for the good of the family. Plain and simple. Got it?"

"Got it," everyone chimed enthusiastically.

"Are you *sure* you got it, Thad?" Nora asked, leaning across her mother to give him her "transparent" stare.

"I have a firmer grip on it than you do," he said. He made a muscle.

"That's not the muscle you need to use." Nora tapped the side of her head. "Try this one for a change. It could use a workout."

"Oh, so now the brain's a muscle? Better check your biology, Nora."

"All right, you two." Mrs. Hartley stood up and fluttered her hands at them briskly, as if rounding up chickens. "Before we totally lose every gain Sophie led the effort for, let's get this cleaned up. John, it's time for bed."

They started clearing the coffee table. "I guess this means no more family job list," John said glumly.

"I'm afraid so." Mr. Hartley rubbed the top of John's head consolingly. "But you can clean out the garage any time you want."

"Way to go, little sister." Thad stuffed the dirty napkins into a glass. "No more job list."

"I guess that's something," Nora agreed.

Coming from Nora, it was a compliment. Sophie jumped at the chance to take advantage of it.

"We can still all clean together," she said eagerly. "We can turn Saturday mornings into family fun time and have pillow fights and Thad can teach us how to dust and—"

"No can do, Soph, sorry," Thad said. "This boy's headed for the state finals. Gotta practice!"

"If you wake me up on Saturday morning, I'll kill you," said Nora.

"Oh, well," Sophie said philosophically as they filed into the kitchen. "At least we can tear up the family job list."

The space where it had been taped to the refrigerator was empty. They heard shouts coming from the mudroom and discovered Mrs. Hartley with her finger in John's mouth, removing the last bits of the job list he'd torn into pieces and had been attempting to swallow.

"That's what spies do when they're captured!" he shouted as she wadded the wet, slimy pieces into a small ball. "You better never get caught by the enemy, Mom!"

"Why would you wish that on the poor enemy?" said Thad. He was rewarded, by his mother, with a wet fly ball on the side of his head.

CHAPTER TEN

"What else are we doing besides spending the night?" Jenna asked on Saturday afternoon as she and Alice dumped their things on Sophie's bed.

"I'm sure Sophie has something planned," Alice said, "don't you, Sophie?"

"No," Sophie said. "It's more fun if we get together and then think of something to do."

"I like it that way, too," Alice admitted. "I was running out of beauty ideas."

"My mother had to cut some of those beads out of my hair, they got so tangled," Jenna said.

"What'd your grandmother say?" Sophie asked.

"She's going to wait until I'm thirteen. She said I'll care about hair then."

"Thirteen." Sophie shuddered. "You don't have a sister who's thirteen," she said. "It's scary. All kinds of weird things happen."

"You make it sound like a horror movie," said Alice.

"Thirteen-year-old boys are pretty horrible, too," said Jenna.

It made them all feel very cheerful, knowing they were still nine and didn't have to face horrible old age for what felt like many years. They sat in a row on the back steps to think up things to do. There was hardly enough time in the afternoon to fit them all in.

First, they put on a play in Mr. Hartley's van. He had cleaned it out, and when he heard what they wanted to do, he hung up a moving pad to act as a curtain. The play roughly involved a queen (Sophie wearing her tiara), whose princess daughter (Maura, being dragged around like a sack of potatoes by her loving nursemaid, Alice) was frequently and noisily rescued from all kinds of vague threats by a brave horse rider, Jenna.

John wanted to be in it, too, as a spy. The girls wouldn't let him, but they did allow him to stand on a box and sell tickets. Mr. and Mrs. Hartley were the only ones in the audience, but they both applauded enthusiastically.

Thad came home as the play was ending. Mr. Hartley told him he had to mow the lawn before he went back out, so he took turns driving Sophie and Alice and Jenna around the yard in a breathtaking display of skills. Alice's face was beet-red with the glory of sitting next to him.

After that, they had a cookout and a formal family-job-list burning that Sophie insisted on. They had to burn a plain piece of paper because John had ruined the real one, but it felt every bit as good to watch it disintegrate into little charred pieces that floated into the sky. Everyone clapped and cheered, even Jenna and Alice. When the last bits of paper had disappeared, Mr. Hartley took the boys to a movie, leaving the house entirely to the girls.

They took turns soaking in lavender bubble

bath in Mrs. Hartley's huge tub, and then applied generous amounts of wonderful-smelling body powder that left their white footprints on the bathroom floor.

As a grand finale, Nora gave them all facials.

"Five dollars for all three of them?" she was saying under her breath to her mother as Mrs. Hartley followed her into the bedroom. "Do you know how much I'd be paid in a real spa?"

"You're *paying* her?" Sophie protested.

"For heaven's sake, Sophie, lie down!" said Mrs. Hartley. "We'll let her experiment on you first, in case your skin turns green." Jenna and Alice giggled.

Sophie lay down on her bed and put her hands on top of her chest. Nora covered her with a towel and pulled her hair away from her face with a terry cloth band, just like a real spa.

"Stop moving your mouth," she commanded as she smeared what felt like cold mud over Sophie's cheeks and nose.

"I can't help it," said Sophie. "It tickles."

"Hold still, or I'll plug up your nose holes." It was a very unprofessional threat. Luckily, Sophie started laughing so hard, Nora had to join her.

"Oh, Sophie, you should see yourself," said Alice and Jenna, giggling.

When Sophie finally got up to look in the mirror, her face was a blue mask with perfect circles for her eyes and mouth. Nora put masque on Alice and Jenna, and then Mrs. Hartley took their picture before they washed it off.

Nora went to spend the night at a friend's so they could use Sophie's and her room. After Mrs. Hartley helped them set up the small TV from the kitchen, she went down to pop them some popcorn. The girls piled all their sleeping bags on the floor between the two beds for Jenna, who said she loved sleeping on the floor.

They ate popcorn and drank soda and watched a movie, and it was with great satisfaction that Sophie could yell, "No boys allowed!" when John jiggled the doorknob.

"You can say that again," said Jenna.

"Some boys aren't so bad," said Alice. "I think Thad's cute."

"Don't start getting all mushy," said Sophie.

"When was I mushy?" asked Alice.

"You're always mushy," said Jenna.

"Mushy, mushy, mushy," said Sophie.

"It sounds so funny, when you say it like that," said Alice.

"The mushy mushroom mushed in the mouse's mouth," said Jenna. "Say it five times, fast."

The more they tried, the funnier it sounded. Mr. Hartley finally had to knock on the door and say, "Time to settle down in there, girls," which sent them into gales of stifled laughter. They buried their faces in their pillows to muffle the sound.

If the success of a slumber party can be measured by the number of times the parents have to knock on the door and tell everyone to be quiet, then Sophie's slumber party was a great success.

———

In the middle of the night, two raccoons ambled across the Hartleys' backyard and stopped at the garbage cans next to the back porch. One of them sniffed around on the ground, looking for scraps, while the other scrambled nimbly up the steps and reached out with its paw for the lid of the closest can.

The bungee cord Thad had stretched across the top was securely fastened under the edge of the lid. On top of it was the pile of bricks Sophie had run out to collect from the garage, in her pajamas, right before she went to bed.

Disappointed and still hungry, the raccoons moseyed down the driveway and out into the street, looking for a house where the people weren't cooperating for the good of the family quite as much as the Hartleys.